Also by Bradley P. Beaulieu:

The Song of the Shattered Sands

TWELVE KINGS IN SHARAKHAI
WITH BLOOD UPON THE SAND*

* * *

OF SAND AND MALICE MADE

*Coming in 2017 from DAW Books

BRADLEY P. BEAULIEU

OF SAND AND MALICE MADE

A Shattered Sands Novel

DAW BOOKS, INC.

DONALD A. WOLLHEIM, FOUNDER
375 Hudson Street, New York, NY 10014
ELIZABETH R. WOLLHEIM
SHEILA E. GILBERT
PUBLISHERS
www.dawbooks.com

First Printing, September 2016
1 2 3 4 5 6 7 8 9

For the fans, the growing cadre who enjoy sailing the sands of the Great Shangazi. This one's for you.

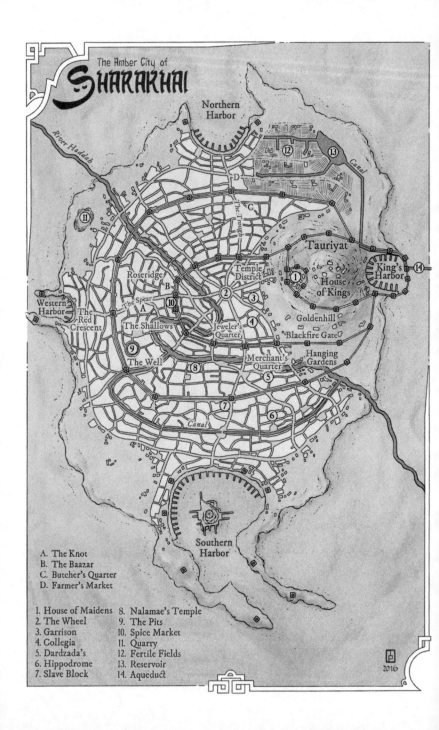

The Amber City of
Sharakhai

Northern Harbor

River Haddah

Tauriyat

King's Harbor

Canal

The Trough

Temple District

House of Kings

Goldenhill

Blackfire Gate

Roseridge

Western Harbor

The Red Crescent

The Spear

The Shallows

Jeweler's Quarter

The Well

Hanging Gardens

Merchant's Quarter

Canal

Southern Harbor

A. The Knot
B. The Baazar
C. Butcher's Quarter
D. Farmer's Market

1. House of Maidens
2. The Wheel
3. Garrison
4. Collegia
5. Dardzada's
6. Hippodrome
7. Slave Block
8. Nalamae's Temple
9. The Pits
10. Spice Market
11. Quarry
12. Fertile Fields
13. Reservoir
14. Aqueduct

2016

OF SAND AND MALICE MADE

Part One

Irindai

ÇEDA FOUND BRAMA by the river.

She watched from within a stand of cattails, where she hunkered low, cool river water lapping at her ankles.

Brama was playing in the water with a dozen other gutter wrens—playing!—apparently without a care in the world after he'd nicked her purse. She felt the anger roiling inside her like a pot boiling over. He'd probably come straight here to brag to his friends, show them what he'd done and challenge them to do the same, then demand tribute like some paltry lord of mud and fleas.

The lot of them were playing skipjack along the Haddah's muddy banks. One by one, boys and girls would run to the lip of the bank and leap onto a grimy piece of canvas pulled taut as a drum by seven or eight of the older children, who would then launch the little ones into the air. They would flail their arms and legs midflight, screaming or yelling, before splashing like stones into the Haddah, water spraying like diamonds in the dry, desert heat.

Lip curling, Çeda watched as Brama was launched in turn. He barked like a jackal and flew through the air to crash into the water, arms and legs spread wide. After, he waded back to the canvas and relieved one of the others so they could make a run of their own—the same pattern he'd followed every other time he'd jumped into the river.

When he reaches dry ground, Çeda told herself.

With a measured pace, Çeda pulled out a locket on a silver chain from inside her dress. She pried the locket open, its two halves spreading like wings to reveal a dried white petal with a tip of palest blue. After taking the petal out, she clipped the locket closed and placed the fragile petal beneath her tongue. Spit filled her mouth. A shiver ran down her frame as the flavor of spices filled her. Mace and rosemary and a hint of jasmine and other things she didn't have words for.

The petal had been stolen from the adichara, a forbidden tree that bloomed only once every six weeks under the light of the twin moons. When gathered on such nights, they were imbued with breathtaking power. Part of her hated to use even one of the petals on Brama, but her anger over what he'd done was more than strong enough to smother any reluctance.

As the effects of the petal spread, granting a barely contained verve to her limbs, she stuffed the locket back inside her dress and scanned the river. Colors were sharper now. She could *hear* more as well, not only the children in the river but the very breath and rattle of the city. It took effort in the early moments of imbibing the petals to concentrate, but she was used to doing so, and she focused her attention on those near and around Brama. A clutch of children were playing downriver, some trying to spear fish, others wading and laughing or splashing one another. Most likely they wouldn't interfere. There was one who gave her pause, though, a dark-skinned Kundhunese boy with bright blue eyes. He stood apart from the others, and seemed to be watching Brama and the children with almost as much interest as Çeda. She would swear she'd seen him before, but just then she couldn't remember where or when it might have been.

She worked at the memory, scratching at it, but like chasing a stubborn sliver it only sank deeper in her mind, and soon Brama was handing over his section of the canvas to a girl with a lopsided grin.

The moment Brama gained the bank, Çeda parted the cattails and marched forward. "Brama!"

He turned, staring at her with a frown. Her identity was still hidden by her white turban and veil, so he wouldn't know who she was, but she could see in his eyes that he recognized the flowing blue dress she'd been wearing early that morning.

He scanned the area to see if anyone else was with her. "What do you want?"

"There's something you stole from me," she called, "and I mean to have it back." Çeda didn't know Brama well. He was a boy who liked to traipse about Sharakhai's west end, bullying some, shying away from others. He was an opportunist and a right good lock-slip if rumor was true. She might have gone all her days and never thought twice about Brama but that morning he'd stolen something from her: a purse she was meant to deliver to Osman—a shade, as it was known in Sharakhai. It was as simple a task as Osman had ever given her—hardly more than a prance across the city—and she'd bungled it, but she'd be damned by Bakhi's bright hammer before she'd let a boy like Brama get away with it.

Brama's eyes flicked to the children in the river. They were watching, not yet approaching, but it wouldn't take long before they came to back him up. The moment his eyes were off her, Çeda drew her shinai, her curved wooden practice sword, from its holder at her belt. She didn't like walking around Sharakhai with a real sword—girls of fifteen, even tall as she was, attracted notice when bearing steel—but few enough spent more than a passing glance at a girl wearing a shinai, especially in the west end where children practicing the dance of blades could be found on any street, alley, or open space one cared to look.

Brama's eyes were only for Çeda now. He looked her up and down, perhaps truly noticing her frame for the first time. She was tall. She had more muscle than he might have noticed earlier. She was holding a sword with a cozy grip—a *lover's* grip, the bladewrights called it, the kind that revealed just how intimate a sword and its master were with one another—and with the magic of the petal now running through her veins, Çeda was itching to use it.

Brama's friends were stepping out of the water now, and it seemed to lend him some confidence, for he swelled, not unlike a man who'd had one too many glasses of araq, or like the dirt dogs in the pits often did when they knew they were outmatched. He stuffed one hand down his still-dripping trousers and pulled out a short but well-edged knife. "I've got nothing of yours"—he smiled as the other children fanned around and behind Çeda—"so why don't you run off before that pretty dress of yours is stained red?"

Brama had muscle as well, but it was the rangy sort, the kind that felt good to thump with the edge of a wooden sword. "You stole a purse, cut from my belt as I strode through the spice market."

"A thousand and one gutter wrens wander that market day and night. Any one of them might have stolen your purse."

"Ah, but it *wasn't* any one of them." She lifted the point of her shinai and thrust it toward Brama's chest. "The nick from your little knife wasn't nearly as clean as you thought, Brama Junayd'ava. I saw you running like a whipped dog down the aisles, and I *know* you heard me calling."

She thought he might be put off by the use of his familial name, but instead he squinted, as if he recognized her voice and was trying to place it. "I don't know who it might have been, but you're a fool if you think it was me."

The circle around her was closing in now, some with river stones clutched in their scrawny hands.

Çeda took a half-step closer to Brama and dropped into a fighting stance. "This is your last warning, Brama."

Brama merely smiled. "You should have run while you had the chance."

Çeda didn't wait any longer. She charged.

She brought her sword swiftly down against his hastily raised defenses. The wooden blade beat with an audible crack against his forearms, then his rib cage, then his knee—not enough to break bones, though she could easily have done so, but certainly enough to send him crumpling to the ground.

Other children rushed in, but if her time in the pits had taught her anything it was how to maintain distance with the enemy, even many at once. She rushed past Brama's fallen form, twisting and striking a girl every bit as tall as Brama across the face. Another came barreling after, but Çeda dropped and snapped her leg out, catching the girl and sending her tumbling off the bank and into the river.

The ones with the stones loosed them at Çeda as two more boys braved the range of her sword. One stone struck a glancing blow against her shoulder, another squarely against her ribs, but the effects of the petal deadened the pain. Four quick strokes of her shinai and the boys were howling away, shaking pain from their knuckles and wrists.

She was alone now. None would come near. Even the boy holding rocks the size of lemons remained still as a statue, the fear plain on his face.

Brama lay at her feet, cringing.

"Where's the purse?" she asked him.

His face grew hard, his teeth gritting away the pain. "I don't have it."

"That wasn't what I asked you, Brama." She grabbed a hunk of his hair—"I said, *where is it?*"—and slammed his head onto the ground.

"*I don't have it!*"

Somehow, his refusal made her go calm as the night's cool winds. She let go of Brama's hair and stood, staring down at him with her shinai still held easily in her right hand. "When are you going to learn, Brama?" She raised her sword, ready to give him something to think about before asking him the question again, but she stopped when she heard a piercing whistle from somewhere along the riverbank. She turned, but not before laying the tip of her sword over Brama's kidney, a warning for him to lie still.

A man with broad shoulders wearing laced sandals and a striped kaftan was standing near the edge of the river, staring at her. The sun glinted brightly off the lattice of shallow waves behind him, so she didn't at first recognize him—and why by the gods' sweet breath would he be here in any case?—but soon she *did* recognize him.

Osman.

The very man she should have delivered the purse to this morning. But she'd failed to, because of fucking Brama.

She was half-tempted to bring the sword down across Brama's thieving little face. He flinched, perhaps sensing the brewing sandstorm within her, and that made her want to strike him even more, but she stayed her hand when Osman shouted, "Enough!" in that clipped tone of his. And then she saw what he was holding in his right hand, dangling like a fish.

The purse. *Her* purse, a small, red leather affair, the

very one he'd asked her to pick up and bring to him at the pits.

"Come," he said, and turned to walk along the dusty bank of the Haddah.

Çeda had no difficulty understanding the command was meant for her, so she left, but not before kicking dirt over Brama's quivering form. As she walked toward Osman, she realized the Kundhunese boy with the blue eyes was watching her intently.

Not Osman. Just her.

"Hurry up," Osman said.

She refused to run, but she quickened her pace until they were walking side by side. She glanced back only once and found that the Kundhunese boy had vanished. She scanned the river, curious, but she was so intrigued by Osman's sudden possession of the purse that she gave up after too long. How by the hot desert winds could Osman have learned not only that the purse had been stolen but that Brama had been the one to do it? And after learning it, how could he have found it so quickly?

The answer came to her in little time, but before she could say anything about it, Osman said, "Why confront him?"

"What?"

"Why challenge Brama while he's playing with his friends along the Haddah?"

Çeda shrugged. "Because I had to know where the purse was."

"You knew where the purse was."

"No, I didn't."

"Yes, you did. I saw you watching him as he hid his clothes and other things in the cattails. You could have taken it while they were splashing in the river."

He'd seen that, had he?

She tried on a dozen different answers, finally settling on, "He deserved it."

"A lot of boys like Brama deserve a beating, but you can't be the one to give it to them, Çeda. People in Sharakhai have long memories, and sooner or later, the city will end up the master and you the student, and I'll wager you're old enough to know how that lesson is likely to end."

"I thought you'd be grateful. It was *your* package I was protecting."

"First of all, the only time you'll find me grateful is when none of my packages go missing. Second, that was no favor you were doling out back there. Not for my benefit, in any case. You were nursing a wound to your precious ego. You fight in the pits, and if I'm being truthful, I've rarely seen someone with the gifts the gods themselves surely bestowed upon you, but don't think that trading blows with dirt dogs helps you at all in the shadows of the streets. You're shrewd enough when you put your mind to it, but you'd better start putting that quality to better use before I find that you've been given back to the desert."

Given back to the desert, a phrase that spoke of bleached bones, of men and women forgotten and swallowed by the Shangazi's ever-shifting dunes. She was so angry she wasn't sure she wouldn't still give *Brama* back to the desert. "You do this to everyone, then?" Çeda asked as a wagon train rumbled past. "Set them up to see how they dance?"

Osman shrugged, not even looking at her. "I had to know what you'd do if you lost a package."

"And?"

"And what?"

"How did I do?"

"Poorly. It's the *package* I care about, Çeda. Let *me* decide who needs a beating and who doesn't. Understand?"

"Yes," she said, forcing the words through her teeth.

Osman stopped walking. They were on a small lane now, a well-worn one used by laborers to head to and from Sharakhai's sandy northern harbor. Men and women passed them by like the Haddah's waters around a pair of particularly surly stones. "Tell me you understand."

She stared into his eyes, ready to answer with another petulant, barking reply, but she stopped herself. This was no small thing he was asking. Osman might have been a pit fighter once, but he was a shademan now. He'd taken Çeda under his wing, but he would toss her to the dogs if he thought he couldn't trust her.

She'd been foolish with Brama. She saw that now. She needed to watch out for Osman's interests, not her own.

"I understand," she said.

"Good, because there's something a bit more delicate we need to discuss."

"*That* doesn't sound good."

Osman shared a wolfish smile and bowed his head like old Ibrahim the storyteller did before beginning a tale. "How astute of you to notice."

They passed out of an alley and onto the cobblestone quay surrounding the northern harbor. A line of eight sandships were just setting sail, their long runners carrying them swiftly over the amber sand toward the gap between the two tall lighthouses. "Two days ago," Osman continued, leading her over a meandering rank of stones that marked the dry yard around the lighthouse, "a man named Kadir came to me. He works for someone who is . . . Well, let's just say she's a powerful woman, indeed. Kadir's visit was regarding a package that was delivered to him three weeks ago, a package delivered by you." Osman came to a stop short of the door to the lighthouse. Beside them lay an old mint garden that years ago had been well-tended but had since lain forgotten, so that its contents looked little better than a forgotten pile of brown twine. "He also claimed that the contents had been poisoned."

Suddenly Çeda felt very, very small. She felt under scrutiny, like a dung beetle crawling over open sand. "Poisoned?"

"Poisoned."

"By whom?"

"That's the question, isn't it?"

"Well, it wasn't me! I remember that package. It was delivered as you asked!"

"I know."

"I didn't tamper with it."

"I *know*, or we'd be having a very different conversation."

"Is this why you had Brama steal the purse?"

Osman waggled his head. "I'd've done it sooner or later." Çeda opened her mouth to deny it again, but Osman held up his hand. "Kadir wishes to speak with you. He believes he knows who sent the poison but would like to find more clues from you if there are any to be found."

Çeda stared deeper into his eyes. "And you told him I

would? What if he thinks I *did* poison the contents? What kind of fool would I be to simply walk into his arms?"

"As I said, he works for a powerful woman. If *she* thought you had done so, she wouldn't have done me the courtesy of having Kadir ask to see you. He and I spoke for a long while. I believe him, Çeda, and you will be under my protection. You'll be safe enough, though I'm sure it won't be a comfortable conversation to have."

"And if I refuse?"

"Then Kadir doesn't get what he wants and life goes on."

"With no repercussions?"

A sad simulacrum of a smile broke over Osman's broad, handsome face. "None for *you*."

"But you would lose her as a client."

Osman shrugged. "In all likelihood, yes."

Çeda took a deep breath. She didn't like this. She didn't like this one bit. She'd known her shading with Osman would get her into some trouble sooner or later. She just hadn't expected it would come from Osman himself. Still, she owed him much, and if this Kadir really *did* wish to speak of clues to the one who'd meddled with the package, then it seemed safe enough.

"Very well," she said.

Osman nodded, then put two fingers to his mouth

and whistled sharply. From the lighthouse came Tariq, a boy Çeda had grown up with and who had joined the ranks of Osman's shades around the same time she had.

"Bring them," Osman said.

Tariq nodded and ran off down the quay before ducking into an alley. Soon, a rich, covered araba led by two horses was trundling up the quay toward the lighthouse with Tariq hanging off the back. When it had swung around the sandy circle in the yard and pulled to a stop, Tariq dropped and ran back to stand in the lighthouse doorway. Osman swung the araba's door open and Çeda climbed inside.

"Come see me when it's done," Osman said, closing the door and knocking twice upon it. "I'll stay until you return."

As the araba pulled away, Çeda saw someone standing on one of the empty piers in the sandy harbor—again, the Kundhunese boy with the bright blue eyes. He had a scar running near his left eye and down his cheek. Strange she hadn't noticed it before, as it was long and puckered in places. The pier and the boy were both lost from sight as the araba passed a long train of wagons loaded high with cord after cord of bright white wood. When the wagons had passed, the boy had vanished.

In a tastefully appointed room Çeda sat in a high-backed chair of ornamented silk. The estate where she found herself had surely been built centuries before. She could tell not only from the architecture, but from the paintings on the walls, the vases on their pedestals, the occasional weapon. They were elegant, all, but had clearly been born of another age.

Ashwandi, the beautiful, dark-skinned woman who'd led Çeda here, lingered in the arched doorway, staring at Çeda with a strange mixture of piqued curiosity and contempt. "Kadir will see you soon," she said in a thick accent, and bowed her head. No sooner had she left than a slender man strode in scanning a sheet of vellum. As he swept behind an opulent desk, Çeda stood and bowed her head, for this was surely Kadir. He ignored her, his eyes continuing to skim the tightly scripted words while holding his free hand at attention behind his back, the pose a steward would often take while standing at attention. His brow creased as he finished. Only then did he set the vellum down and regard Çeda with a critical eye. He hid a frown as he took her in. "Osman sent you?"

This was a man who took his position seriously, Çeda could tell, and it made her even more curious to know who his mistress was. "He did."

"It was you who delivered the package, then?"

"Yes."

"Your name?"

"Çedamihn Ahyanesh'ala."

He nodded as if knowing her full name had incrementally raised her status in his eyes. "Osman was to tell you our purpose here. Did he?"

"To a degree."

A frown appeared on Kadir's refined face. "Tell me what he told you."

"That the package I delivered had been poisoned. That it had been discovered in time. That I was not under suspicion."

"The first two I'll grant you. As to the third"—he swept the back of his damask coat as he sat—"let us see what we see."

Çeda bowed her head once more. "Forgive me if I overstep my bounds, *hajib*, but my master informed me that I had come to help you find the one responsible. Was he mistaken?"

Kadir gave her the smallest of smiles, but it seemed genuine. "He said you were direct."

"My mother always told me there's little point in tarrying when a hare needs chasing."

"There are times when that's *exactly* what needs to happen, but your mother was wise. So tell me, do you remember much from that day?"

Çeda shrugged noncommittally. "I remember it, but

I recall nothing amiss. I came for the box at Osman's estate at nightfall as he'd bid me and, after the moons had set and full night had come, brought it to the drop near Blackfire Gate."

"Did you notice anyone following you?"

"No, or I would have delayed and come the following night."

"Did you notice anything strange in the days before the drop?"

Her mind went immediately to the strange, blue-eyed Kundhuni boy. She remembered where she'd seen him now: at the spice market just before Brama had nicked her purse. She'd seen him again at the river, and then a short while ago at the harbor. How many times had she missed him? Had he been watching her for days? Weeks?

"What is it?" Kadir asked, his dark eyes suddenly sharper.

"It's nothing to do with your package. At least, I don't think it is."

"Just tell me."

"There was a boy. I've seen him several times these past few days."

"He's been following you?"

Çeda shrugged. "I suppose he must have been, though I have no idea why. I've never seen him before."

Kadir seemed eminently unfazed. "He's a head and a half shorter than I, with closely shorn hair and cinnamon skin and bright blue eyes. And a scar"—he ran his little finger down the left side of his face, neatly bisecting the skin between temple and eye—"just here."

"Yes . . . But how did you know?"

Kadir pursed his lips, staring down at the desk for a moment, then he took in Çeda anew, his eyes roaming her form, lingering not only on her face, but on her hands as well, which were riddled with small scars from her time in the pits. She balled them into fists and held them by her side, which only seemed to draw *more* notice to her scars. Kadir smiled a patronizing smile. "The boy you saw is from Kundhun, and the poison on the package you delivered was not meant for my mistress, but for Ashwandi, the woman who delivered you to this room."

Ashwandi had been beautiful, but she had also eyed Çeda uncharitably from the moment she'd stepped foot in the estate.

"Why?" Çeda asked.

"My mistress hosts social gatherings, and in these she has had cause to take on protégés. In her wisdom she took on a Kundhuni girl named Kesaea, a princess of the thousand tribes. Years ago Kesaea had come to Sharakhai with her sister, Ashwandi, and here the two of them have remained, vying for my mistress's attentions. When Kesaea left our employ, there was some, shall we say, *acrimony* over the decision."

"She was forced from her lofty position."

Kadir nodded, granting her the smallest of smiles. "Just so, and as you may have guessed, Ashwandi took her place. You can see how this might have caused more than a little strife between siblings, especially one—may my mistress forgive me for saying it—as petulant as Kesaea."

"But to poison her own sister?"

Kadir shrugged. "Surely you've heard worse stories in the smoke houses of Sharakhai."

In point of fact, she doubted Kadir would be caught dead in a Sharakhani smoke house. "Yes, but from a princess?"

"Are not those who wield the scepter most likely to strike?"

"I suppose," Çeda said. "What of the boy, though? Why should I still find him following me?"

She left unsaid the fact that the boy had likely been following her for quite some time, a logical conclusion that bothered her greatly, not merely for the fact that she hadn't noticed him before today, but because she hadn't a clue as to the reason behind it. If she was to become the unwitting accomplice to this boy's plans, why follow her at all and give Çeda the chance to become wise to it? And for that matter, how would they even have known that she would be the one to take the shade from Osman that night?

Kadir steepled his fingers. "Now that *does* give me pause. Have you no guesses of your own?"

Çeda shrugged. "None," she said. And then the strangest thing happened. A moth flew into Çeda's field of vision. Where it had come from she had no idea, but it landed on her sleeve and sat there, wings fanning slowly. The top of its wings were the deepest indigo Çeda had ever seen, with a bright orange mark akin to a candle flame. Çeda was loath to shoo it away, partly from the sheer surprise of it, but more so from the realization that Kadir was staring at it as if it were about to burst into flame and take Çeda with it.

"They're called irindai," Kadir said with an ease that made Çeda's hackles rise. "Some call them cressetwings, and consider what just happened to you a sign of bountiful luck."

"Others call them gallows moths," she replied, "and consider them a sign of imminent death."

"Well," he said, standing and motioning to the way out, "as with so much in the world, surely the truth lies somewhere in between." As Çeda stood, the moth flew away and was lost in the fronds of a potted fern in the corner. "I'll only ask you for one more thing. Keep an eye out for the boy. I would not recommend you approach him—there's no telling how Kesaea might have armed him—but if you discover that he's following you still, return to this estate and inform me."

Çeda might have granted Kadir that if she'd been planning to leave this matter alone, but she refused to allow some Kundhuni child to use her as his plaything. She couldn't tell that to Kadir, though, not leastwise because it might get back to Osman, so she nodded obediently and said, "Very well."

As Kadir joined her at the arched entryway, he held his hands out to her, as if asking her to dance. It was such an odd and unexpected gesture that she complied, lifting her hands for him to take. He did, then considered her with deliberate care. "They say scars have tales to tell, each and every one." He examined not just her hands, but her face, her body, her legs, even her ankles, which somehow made her feel unclothed. "What would yours tell, Çedamihn Ahyanesh'ala?"

"Tales are not told for free in this city, my lord."

"If it's money you want"—he leaned toward her—"you need but whisper the price."

"The price of their telling is something you cannot afford."

Kadir laughed. "You'd do well not to underestimate

the size of my mistress's purse, nor her will to follow a scent once she's gotten wind of it."

"My tales are my own," she said finally.

For a moment, Kadir seemed prepared to press her, but then he raised her hands and bowed his head. "Forgive my boldness. A habit most foul, formed from years of service."

"Think nothing of it," Çeda said, though somehow she doubted he would heed her words. No matter what he said, his eyes were too hungry, too expectant of submission.

Kadir raised his hand high and motioned to Ashwandi, who stood farther down the hall. She came and put on a smile, motioning for Çeda to follow her. Her smile vanished, however, when the moth fluttered out from Kadir's office to flitter around the two of them. As they walked toward the entrance to the estate, the moth continued to dog them, and it became clear it was fluttering around Çeda much more than it was Ashwandi, a thing that appeared to please the Kundhunese woman not at all.

The clack from the strike of wooden swords filled the desert air, strangely deadened by the surrounding dunes where Çeda and Djaga, her mentor in the pits, fought.

The sun shined off Djaga's dark, sweat-glistened skin. The sand shushed as they glided over it, a strangely calming sound amidst the rattle of armor and the thud of their shinai as they engaged then backed away.

Çeda fought with abandon, hoping to impress, pushing herself more than she had in a long while. When Djaga retreated, Çeda closed the gap. When Djaga pressed, Çeda countered as soon as the flurry had ended. When Djaga ran backward, Çeda flew after her. She thought she'd timed her advance perfectly, but just as she was lunging forward, Djaga did too, beating aside her blade and sending a nasty swipe of her shinai over Çeda's thigh.

Çeda, thinking Djaga was going to press her advantage, slid quickly away as the pain blossomed, but instead the tall black woman stopped and stood, chest heaving, her face a sneer of disgust. "You invite me to spar," she said in an accent similar but distinctly different from Ashwandi's, "and this is what I get? You're not watching *me*."

Çeda opened her mouth to explain, to apologize, but Djaga abruptly turned away and headed for the skiff they'd sailed that morning from Sharakhai's western harbor. Together they stepped over the runners of the sand-ship to reach the ship's side, at which point Djaga leaned over the gunwales, pulled the cork from their keg of water, and filled a gourd cup. "You're distracted," Djaga said after downing the cup and running the back of her hand over her mouth. She refilled the cup and held it out for Çeda. "Why?"

There was no sense denying it. She *was* distracted. Çeda took the cup and drank down the sun-warmed water.

"Tell me it's a man," Djaga went on, a smile making her full lips go crooked. "Tell me you've decided to take your Emre to bed. He's disappointed you, hasn't he? I knew he would. Haven't I always said it? No man as gorgeous as that knows his way to the promised land."

Çeda laughed. She shared a home with Emre, and he meant much to her, but not *that*—they'd probably never be *that*—yet it never stopped Djaga from digging her sharp elbows into Çeda's ribs every chance she got.

"Come, come. What's there to think about? He's a pretty boy . . . You're a pretty girl. . . ."

"Well, if you must know," Çeda said, desperate to move the conversation beyond these particular grounds, "it *is* about a boy."

"A boy . . ."

"A Kundhunese boy."

"Well, well, well . . . A *Kundhunese* boy . . . Who knew it was the *darker* berries that tempted your palate?" Djaga laughed, then bowed and flourished her arms to the desert around them. "Know this, oh Çeda the White Wolf. The desert, she is wide enough to hold all your secrets and more. Tell us both your tale if you're bold enough."

Gods, where to begin? In the days that followed her meeting with Kadir, she would swear by her mother's own blood that she'd seen the blue-eyed boy a half-dozen times, but always from the corner of her eye. Always, when she looked with a direct gaze, she found someone or some*thing* else entirely—boys or even girls with similarly dark skin, lighter-skinned boys wearing dark clothes, even the simple swaying of shadows beneath the odd acacia tree. Once she thought she'd spotted him in the ceaseless flow of traffic along the Trough, but when she'd caught up to him and spun him around, it had been a Sharakhani boy with closely shorn hair who looked nothing like the bright-eyed Kundhuni. The mother had shoved Çeda away and shouted with rage. Under the angry glares of those standing nearby, Çeda had retreated, wondering what was happening to her.

She'd spent the next few days wallowing in confusion and fear while a small voice whispered from the corners of her mind—*you're going mad, mad, mad, you're going mad*. A fury born from her own helplessness grew hotter by the day, but what good was fury when there was nothing to direct it against? She needed a change. If the winds were blowing across one's bow, one didn't simply stay the course. One turned and tacked until the safety of port was reached once more. And who better to help steer this strange ship than Djaga? So much of this tale seemed to be wrapped up in the people of Kundhun, their customs, their norms, and Djaga was Kundhunese. She might see any number of things Çeda was blind to. So she told Djaga her tale. She spoke of the shade, of Osman's confession after, of her visit with Kadir. She spent a long while describing the strange blue-eyed boy with the cinnamon skin, hoping Djaga would somehow know him, but there was no glimmer of recognition in her eyes. She described Ashwandi as well, receiving only a halfhearted shrug in reply.

When she was done, she asked Djaga, "Have you heard of her, this princess Kesaea?"

"No," Djaga replied, "but you know what we say in the backlands. If you stand our princesses shoulder to shoulder with our princes, they will drown the land like blades of grass."

It was true. There were as many kings and queens as there were hills in Kundhun, or so it seemed. "It was so strange," Çeda went on. "When I left, a moth followed me."

Djaga smiled her broad smile. "Good luck be upon you."

But Çeda shrugged. "So they say, but it was a gallows moth."

"An irindai? A cressetwing?"

"Yes. Why are you making that face?"

"Who did you say is this Kadir's mistress?"

"I was never told her name."

Djaga's expression pinched from one of confusion to outright worry. "There's a woman who hides in the shadows of the powerful in Sharakhai. A drug lord named Rümayesh. Have you heard the name?"

"I've heard it," Çeda lied.

"I can tell you don't know enough, girl. Not nearly enough. Those who enter her house pay fistfuls of rahl to do so—not the silver of the southern quarter, mind you, nor the coppers of the west end, but *gold*. Her clientele is exclusive. The lords and ladies of Goldenhill, those of noble blood, rich merchants and caravan masters who paid their way into Rümayesh's good graces, and in return she feeds them dreams, dreams she summons and all share in. Dreams taken from the souls that Rümayesh herself selects."

"What makes you think Rümayesh has anything to do with this?"

Djaga's face was staring out at the sand, her eyes distant, but now she pulled her gaze away and stared down at Çeda. "Because she uses irindai, Çedamihn."

Someone, somewhere danced a dance right over Çeda's grave. She was just about to ask, *How can you know?*, when Djaga went on.

"Years ago there was a woman in the pits, a dirt dog who taught me as I teach you now. Her name was Izel, and one day she disappeared. For weeks we searched for her. She was found at the bottom of a dry well two months later, still alive, the crushed body of a cressetwing stuffed inside her mouth. We nursed her back to health, but she was never the same. Her mind was gone. She remembered nothing—not why or where she'd been taken, nor who had taken her. She couldn't even remember who she was, not much of it, anyway. It had all been taken from her. She did whisper a name, though, over and over."

"Rümayesh."

"Just so, girl. She took her own life two months later"—Djaga drew her thumb across her neck—"a crimson smile, drawn with her favorite sword." She looked Çeda up and down as if she were in danger even here in the desert. "You say he's left you alone, this Kadir?"

"As near as I can tell."

"Then make no mistake, the gods of the desert shine upon you!" Djaga took the gourd cup from Çeda and set it onto the keg. In unspoken agreement, they strode away from the skiff and began loosening their limbs. "Watch yourself in the days ahead, and when we return to Sharakhai, go to Bakhi's temple. Give him a kind word and show him a bit of silver, or gold if you can manage, lest he take it all back."

Çeda had no intention of doing so—she didn't believe in filling the coffers of the temples any more than she believed in giving the Kings of Sharakhai their due respect—but she nodded just the same.

"Now come!" Djaga brought her blade quickly down across Çeda's defenses, a swing Çeda beat aside easily. "You've a bout in two weeks." She swung again, and again Çeda blocked it, backing up this time. "People know we spar with one another, girl." A third strike came, a thing Djaga put her entire body into, but Çeda skipped back, avoiding the blow. "I'll not have it said the White Wolf is some poor imitation of the Lion of Kundhun!"

Çeda retreated and bowed, arms and shinai swept back while her eyes were fixed on Djaga. "Very well," she said, and leapt in for more. For a short while, there in the desert, her troubles were lost in the spindrift and the fury of their blows.

The days passed quickly after that.

Çeda saw the boy again—several times, in fact, and now she was certain it was him. Once, she'd nearly trapped him in the Well, the quarter of the city that held Osman's pits. She'd chased after him, yelling for him to stop, her hand nearly upon him, but when she'd turned the corner, she found the alley ahead empty. At a whistle, she'd craned her head back and found him three stories up, staring down at her with a wide, jackal smile. And then he was gone, leaving a knot inside her she couldn't untie, a knot composed of anger and impotence and foolishness.

He must be a warlock, she decided—it ran thick in some areas of Kundhun—and now for some reason he was toying with her. She vowed to find him, but for the life of her she had no idea how she would manage it. Every time she tried to lie in wait, she ended up spending hours with nothing to show for it.

Instead she lost herself in preparations for her upcoming bout—running in the mornings, sparring in the afternoons, lifting Djaga's stone weights beneath the pier in the western harbor in the evenings. Osman had told her she'd have no shading work until after her day in the pits, a thing that bothered her at first, but given that there was nothing she could do about it she threw herself into her training with an abandon she hadn't felt in months.

Djaga noticed, and even allowed a grudging nod once or twice for how focused Çeda's technique had become. "Good, girl. Good. Now keep your rage bottled up.

Release it in the pits, not before. It's not so hard as you might think."

Çeda thought she understood, but as the day of her bout approached, she found herself becoming more and more anxious, not from any fear over her opponent—a Mirean swordmaster who'd had some small amount of success in the pits—but from the relentless feeling that she was being watched. Whether by some trick of the mind or the unseen workings of the boy, she felt on display, a prized akhala being paraded before auction. All across the city, men, but more often women, were spying her out. She was sure of it. And yet whenever she looked, they were doing completely innocent things, apparently oblivious to her presence.

The experience so unnerved her that, despite her distaste over it, she took Djaga's advice and went to Bakhi's temple and dropped three golden coins into the alms basket at the foot of Bakhi's altar. She thought to speak with the priestess, but the old, bent woman had stared down at Çeda's kneeling form with such a sour expression that Çeda had immediately stood and left the temple.

Soon, all the confidence she'd built while training with Djaga began to erode. "Enough," Djaga said two days before the match. "We've practiced enough. Too much, in fact. There are times when you can overtrain, and I think I've done it with you, girl. Take this time before your match. Stay away from the pits, think of anything but fighting, and you'll return a new woman."

"And if I don't?"

"Then you'll be no worse off than you are now. You're in your mind too much. Go to your Emre. Fuck him like you should have done long ago. Or take another to your bed. But for the love of the gods, let your sword lay untouched."

Near dusk that evening, as Çeda wended her way through the tents of the bazaars, waving to those who had remained throughout the dinner hours hoping to catch a final few patrons, she felt someone new watching her: a woman who Çeda could tell was thin and lithe but little more, for her head was hidden in a deep cowl, her hands within the long, flowing sleeves. Çeda had no idea who the woman might be, but she wasn't about to lead her toward the home she shared with Emre.

She kept her pace, moving along a narrow street that ran down toward the slums of the Shallows. When she came to the next corner and turned, she ducked into an elaborate stone archway: the entrance to a boneyard that looked as though it had stood longer than Sharakhai itself.

She glanced over the yard for the telltale glow of wights or wailers—one didn't treat boneyards lightly in the desert—then peered out through the arch from behind a stone pillar marking one of the graves. She saw the form soon enough, a shadow in the deeper darkness. The woman slowed, perhaps realizing she'd lost her quarry. She pulled her cowl off her head and turned this way, then that, then continued down the street.

It was too dark to see her clearly from this distance, but Çeda knew it was Ashwandi, the woman who'd taken her to speak with Kadir, who'd led her out of the estate when they were done. What by Tulathan's bright eyes would she be doing chasing Çeda through the streets? And why was she doing it so clumsily?

Çeda drew the knife from her belt and followed, padding carefully in time with Ashwandi's footsteps but with broader strides, until she was right behind her. Ashwandi turned, eyes wide as she raised her hands to fend Çeda off, but she was too late. In a blink Çeda had slipped her arm around Ashwandi's neck and pressed the tip of her knife into her back—not enough to draw blood, but certainly enough to make Ashwandi intimately familiar with just how sharp Çeda's blades were kept.

"You might get away with such things east of the Trough," Çeda whispered, "but not here." She pressed the knife deeper, enough to pierce skin, drawing a gasp from Ashwandi. "Here, women like you are as likely to end up on the banks of the Haddah staring sightless into a star-filled sky as they are to make it home again."

"I'm not the one you should be worried about," she rasped.

"No?" Çeda asked, easing her hold on Ashwandi's throat. "Who, then? Your mistress, Rümayesh?"

"I am no *servant* of Rümayesh! I am her love, and she is mine." Her Kundhunese accent was noticeable, but more like a fine bottle of citrus wine than the harsh, home-brewed araq of Djaga's accent.

"She's after me, isn't she? That's why I'm being followed."

"You begin to understand, yes? But I tell you, you have no idea the sort of trouble you're in."

Çeda shoved her away. It was then that Çeda realized that a bandage was wrapped tightly around Ashwandi's left hand. With a pace that spoke of self-consciousness, or even embarrassment, she used her good hand to tug her sleeve back over the bandage, then pulled her cowl back into place. Only when her face was hidden within its depths did she speak once more. "Do you know who Rümayesh is? She has *seen* you, girl. She is *intrigued* . . . Nothing will draw her attention away now, not until she tires of you."

Çeda felt suddenly exposed and foolish, a fly caught in a very intricate web. "What would she want of *me*?"

"You're a tasty little treat, I'll give you that. She's taken by this girl who shades at night but fights in the pits by light of day." Even in the dying light, Çeda was sure Ashwandi caught her surprised expression. "Yes, she knows of your *other* pursuits with Osman, and now

37

she's taken by the pretty thing that came to her estate, by the White Wolf who sank her fangs into the Malasani brute."

This implied much . . . That Rümayesh likely knew of Çeda's time with Djaga, her training for her coming bout, her time in the pits, perhaps. Çeda didn't merely feel off-balance; she felt like the world had been tipped upside down, and now the city was crashing down around her. "I came to Kadir to speak of a *package*. That was all."

"You've been set up, child, as have I."

Brandishing her knife, Çeda closed the distance between them with one long stride. "Make some bloody sense before I rethink how very nice I've been treating you."

"Kadir told you of my sister, Kesaea. For years *she* held the favored position at Rümayesh's side, longer than any other, if the stories I've heard are true. But Rümayesh grew tired of her, as I knew she would, and *I* stepped into her place." Ashwandi shrugged. "Kesaea was angry. With Rümayesh, with me. But after a week of her typical petulance, she returned home to Kundhun, and I hoped that would be the end of it."

"But it wasn't, was it? *She* sent the boy."

"Boys. There are two of them. Twins. And she didn't *send* them. She *summoned* them. Our mother has the blood of witches running through her veins, and Kesaea inherited much of it. Their names are Hidi and Makuo. Hidi is the angry one. He has a scar running down his cheek, a remnant of the one and only time he disobeyed his father, the trickster god, Onondu, our god of vengeance in the savannah lands."

By the desert's endless sand, *twins* . . . And born of a trickster god. It explained, perhaps, why she'd been unable to do any more than see them from the corner of her eye. They'd been toying with her all along. "But why?" Çeda asked. "What would those boys want with me?"

Ashwandi looked at her as if she were daft. "Don't you see? They were sent by my sister to harm *me*. They've been sent to find a way for me to fall from grace, and in you, they've found it, for if Rümayesh becomes entranced with you . . ."

"She'll what, forget about you?"

Ashwandi shrugged. "It is her way. There isn't room in her life for more than one obsession."

"You wish to be that? An obsession?"

"You don't know what it's like . . . It's wondrous when she turns her gaze upon you, if you don't fight it, that is. To be without it . . ."

Çeda's head was swimming. "Tell Rümayesh what your sister has done! Surely she'll see that she's being manipulated."

"I have." Ashwandi turned, as if worried someone was watching. "But it isn't Rümayesh who's being manipulated. It's us. All of us. You, me, Kesaea, even Onondu, which surely pleases her to no end. Don't you see, girl? Rümayesh *enjoys* this, seeing us squabble and fight."

"She acts like a god herself."

Even from within the cowl, Çeda could see Ashwandi's eyes growing intense, and when she spoke once more, her words were very, very soft. "You aren't far from the mark, but there's something you might do."

"Out with it, then."

"The boys, Hidi and Makuo. I know how to bind them."

"And how might you do that?"

Ashwandi reached into her robes. "I've already done it." She held out a small fabric pouch for Çeda to take. "Search for them. And when you are near, use this to send them home."

Çeda stared down at the pouch. "What is it?"

Her only response was to take Çeda's hand in hers—the bandaged one—and forcibly press it into Çeda's palm.

Staring at the bloody bandages around her left hand, Çeda had a guess as to what was inside. "Why don't *you* do it?"

"Because they're not here for me. They're here for Rümayesh, and now you, and they will avoid me when they

40

can, for the blood of my mother runs through my veins as well." She nodded toward the pouch. "Onondu will listen to this, and so will Hidi and Makuo."

Çeda had heard how cruel the gods of the savannah were. They demanded much for their favors. Blood. Fingers. Limbs. Sometimes the lives of loved ones. How desperate Ashwandi must be to do such a thing simply to remain by Rümayesh's side.

No, Çeda realized. This was no fault of Ashwandi, nor even Kesaea, but rather the one they both longed for. How strong the lure of Rümayesh to make them both do this, for surely Kesaea had made a similar bloody sacrifice on her return to Kundhun.

Rümayesh had cast a spell that had utterly bewitched them both, these princesses of Kundhun.

Çeda stuffed the pouch, heavy as a lodestone, into the larger leather bag on her belt. "What do I do?"

"Wear it in their presence. They will listen to you, and they will grant you one favor."

"A *favor*? What am I to do with that? Can I ask them to simply leave?"

"Perhaps, but that would be unwise. They must be turned to Rümayesh now, to make her forget about you. I fear that is the only way for you to survive this."

"And for you to return to her good graces . . ."

Ashwandi shrugged. "We want what we want, and

I've given up much for that to happen." She began stepping away, her eyes still on Çeda. "The twins are drawn to water. You'll find them along the Haddah, often at dusk or dawn."

And then she turned and was gone, swallowed by the growing darkness over Sharakhai.

With the eastern sky a burnished bronze and the stars still shining in the west, Çeda pulled the black veil across her face and crept along the edge of the Haddah, watching carefully for signs of movement along the riverbank. She had arrived hours ago, hoping to catch the godling twins either in the night or as the sun rose. She still hadn't found them, and soon the city would be waking from its slumber. She didn't wish to be skulking along the river when it did, but the desire to find them was palpable as a canker, and every bit as maddening.

The talk with Ashwandi had so shaken Çeda she hadn't gone home last night, preferring to sleep in a hammock at the rear of Ibrahim the storyteller's tiny mudbrick home. She'd unwrapped the rolled bandage and found Ashwandi's severed finger resting there with a leather cord running through it like some depraved version of thread and needle. She'd held it up to the starry sky, looked at it beneath the light of the moons, Rhia and

Tulathan, wondering if she would feel the magic bound to it, or through it that of the twin boys. She'd felt nothing, though, and after a time she'd slipped the cord over her neck and worn the finger like a talisman, which was surely what Ashwandi had meant for her to do.

It rested between her breasts, a thing she was all too conscious of, especially when she walked. It tickled her skin like the unwelcome touch of a man, and she longed to be rid of it, but she couldn't, she knew. Not until this was all over.

She parted the reeds and padded farther down the Haddah. She passed beneath a stone bridge, looking carefully along its underside, which was more than large enough for the boys to hide in, but when she found nothing she moved on, heading deeper into the city.

Above her, beyond the banks, a donkey brayed. A woman shouted at it, and the sounds of a millstone came alive, dwindling and then replaced by burble of the river and the rattle of stones as Çeda trekked onward. The sky brightened further. Carts clattered over bridges. Laborers trudged along, their lunches bundled in cloth. A boy and a girl, both with wild, kinky hair, headed down to the banks of the Haddah with nets in hand. She even saw one of the rare Qaimiri trading ships rowing toward a pier, her lateen sails up, catching a favorable wind.

But of the twins she saw no sign.

She was just about ready to give up when she saw movement near an old acacia. Half the branches were dead, and the thing looked as though it were about to tip over and fall in the water at any moment. But in the branches still choked with leaves she could see two legs hanging down, swinging back and forth. The skin was the same dark color she remembered, and when she looked harder, she saw movement in the branches above—the second twin, surely, sitting higher than the first.

She took to the damp earth along the edge of the bank to silence her footsteps, then pulled her kenshar from its sheath at her belt, whispering a prayer to fickle Bakhi as she did so. Reaching past her mother's silver chain and locket, she slipped Ashwandi's severed finger from around her neck, whipping the leather cord around her hand with one quick snap of her wrist.

She stood twenty paces away now.

As she approached the godling boys, she wondered how vengeful the god Onondu might be. She hoped it wouldn't come to bloodshed, but she'd promised herself that if they wouldn't listen to her commands, she would do whatever she needed to protect herself, even if it meant killing his children. Her identity was her most closely guarded secret, after all—no different than a chest of golden rahl, a chest these boys had tipped over with their mischief, spilling its treasure over the dirt for Rü-mayesh and Ashwandi and perhaps all of Sharakhai to see. Things would only grow worse if she let these boys be.

Ten paces away.

Then five.

The nearest twin faced away from her, looking down-river to the trading ship, which was just mooring, men and women busying themselves about the deck, a few jumping to the pier. She'd grab him first, drag him down and put her knife to his throat, then she'd grip the finger tightly and speak her wish. The moment she took a step forward, though, something snapped beneath her foot.

She glanced down. Gods, a dried branch off the aca-cia. How could she have missed it?

When she looked up once more, Hidi, the one with the scar, was turned on the branch, looking straight at her with those piercing blue eyes. His form blurring, he dropped and sprinted up the bank.

Çeda ran after him and was nearly on him, hand out-stretched, ready to grab a fistful of his ivory-colored tunic, when something fell on her from behind. She col-lapsed and rolled instinctively away, coming to a stand with her kenshar at the ready, but by the time she did both of the boys were bounding away like a brace of des-ert hare.

She was up and chasing them in a flash. "Release me!" she called, gripping Ashwandi's finger tightly. "Do you hear me? I command you to release me!"

But they didn't listen, and soon they were leading a chase into the tight streets of the Knot, a veritable maze of mudbrick that had been built, and then built *upon* so that walkways and homes stretched out and over the street, making Çeda feel all the more watched as men and women and boys stared from the doorways and windows and balconies of their homes.

Çeda sprinted through the streets, wending this way, then that, coming ever closer to reaching the boys. She reached for the nearest of them—her hands even brushed his shoulder—but just then a rangy cat with eyes the very same color of blue as the boys' came running out from behind a pile of overturned crates and tripped her. She fell hard onto the dirt as the boys ahead giggled.

She got up again, her shoulders aching in pain, and followed them down an alley. When she reached the mouth of the alley, however, she found not a pair of twin boys, but a strikingly beautiful woman wearing a jeweled abaya with thread-of-gold embroidery along cuff and collar and hem. She looked every bit as surprised as Çeda— almost as if she too had been following someone through the backtracked ways of the Knot.

"Could it be?" the woman asked, her voice biting as

the desert wind. "The little wren I've been chasing these many weeks?"

Çeda had never seen this woman before—tall, elegant, the air of the aristocracy floating about her like a halo—but her identity could be no clearer than if she'd stated her name from the start.

"I'm no one," she said to Rümayesh.

"Ah, but you are, sweet one." From the billowing sleeve of her right arm a sling dropped into her hand. In a flash she had it spinning over her head, the sound of its blurred passage mingling with Rümayesh's next words. "You certainly are."

Then she released the stone.

Or Çeda *thought* it was a stone.

It flew like a spear for Çeda's chest, and when it struck, a blue powder burst into the cool morning air. She tried not to breathe it, but she'd been startled and took in a lungful of the tainted air. As she spun away, its scent and taste invaded her senses—fresh figs mixed with something acrid, like lemons going to rot.

Çeda turned to run, but she'd not gone five strides before the ground tilted up and struck her like a maul. The world swam in her eyes as she managed with great effort to roll over. Blinking to clear her eyes of their sudden tears, she stared up at the blue sky peeking between the shoulders of the encroaching mudbrick homes. In the windows, old women and a smattering of children watched, but when they recognized the woman approaching Çeda, they ducked their heads back inside and shuttered their windows.

Çeda's kenshar was gone, fallen in the dusty street two paces away, though it might as well have been two leagues for all her leaden limbs would obey her. She'd somehow managed to keep Ashwandi's finger, though; its leather cord had surely prevented it from flying away like her knife. Her throat convulsed. Her tongue was numb, but she chanted while gripping the finger as tightly as her rapidly weakening muscles would allow. "Release me, Hidi . . . Release me, Makuo . . . release me, Onondu . . ."

The only answer she received was the vision of the beautiful woman coming to stand over her, staring down with bright eyes and a wicked demon grin.

Çeda woke staring at the ceiling of a dimly lit room.

She was lying on something cold and hard. She tried to sit up, tried to *move* but was unable to. Her legs felt as though the entire world were pressing down on them. Her arms were little better. Even her eyes moved with a strange listlessness, brought on, no doubt, by the powder that had erupted when the sling stone had struck.

The light in the room flickered strangely.

No.

The ceiling itself . . .

It was covered in some strange cloth, undulating like the fur-covered skin of some curious beast.

No.

Not cloth . . .

Wings. By the gods who breathe, they were *wings*.

She was lying in a room, and above her, covering the ceiling as far as the lamplight revealed, moths blanketed its surface, their wings folding slowly in and out, flashing their bright, cresset-shaped flames over and over and over. They did so in concert such that waves appeared to roll across their surface, as if they were not thousands upon thousands of individuals at all, but a collective that together formed some larger, unknowable consciousness. She couldn't take her eyes from them, so hypnotic were they, not even when she heard footsteps approaching, the sound of them strangely deadened.

It was cool here. And humid. She was underground, then, in a cellar, perhaps, or one of the many caverns that could be found beneath the surface of Sharakhai.

The footsteps came nearer. "Do you like them?"

Rümayesh.

Soon the tall woman was standing over Çeda, staring down with an expression not so different from what a caring mother might share with her sick daughter. The urge to reject the very notion that this woman held any similarities whatsoever to Çeda's mother, Ahya, manifested in a lifting of Çeda's arm in an attempt to slap the look away. Her right arm shifted, but no more, leaving Çeda to fume as Rümayesh reached down and brushed Çeda's hair from her forehead.

"They're wondrous things," she said, looking up to the ceiling, to the walls around them, every surface awash in a landscape of slowly beating wings. "Do you know what they do?"

Çeda tried to respond, but her mouth and tongue felt thick and rigid, like hardening clay.

Rümayesh went on, apparently unfazed by Çeda's silence. "They are taken by the mouth, eaten, in a manner of speaking, and when one does, she is changed, drawn into the whole of the irindai, drawn into a dream of their, and your, making. Some think they're connected, all of them, anywhere in the world, like threads in a grand weave, though I doubt it goes so far as that. These, though . . . My lovely brood . . ." She stopped near the wall and stretched out her forefinger until one of the moths crawled upon it, then she walked slowly across the room until she stood once more at Çeda's side. "*They* are certainly aware of one another, as you will soon see."

"Wuh . . ." Çeda tried forming words. "Wuh . . . Wuh . . ."

Rümayesh stared at the moth as if she hadn't heard Çeda's graceless attempts at speech. "The effects of the powder will wear off in time, certainly soon enough for you to select the irindai you wish to consume"—she flicked her hand and the moth took wing, fluttering in the air for a moment, circling her, then flying back and returning to the very same location it had roosted before crawling onto Rümayesh's outstretched finger—"though if experience has taught me anything, it's the irindai that choose *you*, not the other way around.

"Relax, now. The ritual will start soon. I'd ask that you choose a memory for us to share. My patrons wait years to partake of someone as captivating as you, so choose well. Make the memory dear. I wouldn't want them to leave disappointed." She strode away, heading for the arched entrance to the room. "And I hope you're not thinking of denying me this small request. If you refuse, I'll simply find one on my own, but it's less special for my patrons when I do. The memory is dimmed. More importantly to you, the experience will, I'm afraid, leave your mind quite ravaged, possibly beyond repair."

When she reached the archway, she stopped and turned until she was staring sidelong at Çeda. "Perhaps the tale of the White Wolf's first bout in the pits. Yes, I think that would please them a great deal. There will be plenty of time for the rest in the coming weeks."

Dear gods, it was true then. It was all true. Rümayesh was going to force her to take one of these moths and relive her past. Like a dream, except her *patrons* would dream them as well. How many? A dozen? Two dozen? They'd witness her trips out to the blooming fields to harvest adichara petals. They'd see how she dried them and used them in service of Osman's shades or her own needs. Either was a high crime in Sharakhai, punishable by death. She didn't wish to die, but she was horrified by the thought of someone forcibly taking her memories from her. By Tulathan's bright eyes, would she still have them when the moths were done with her? Or would the experience leave her some useless husk like Djaga's mentor, Izel? Would she go to the farther fields not knowing her mother? She couldn't bear it. She'd lost her mother eight years ago, but at least she still had her *memories* of her. At least she'd *know* her when they were reunited in the world beyond.

And all that wasn't even the worst part.

The Kings of Sharakhai had killed her mother. She had vowed her revenge. It had driven her to so much. Her bouts in the pits, her shading for Osman, her trips to the blooming fields and her endless search for clues of how she could fulfill her promise to knock the wicked Kings from their perches atop this city. But if Rümayesh had her way, all that would be lost like bones ground to dust beneath the dunes of the Great Shangazi.

As a door somewhere boomed shut, Çeda commanded her muscles to move. She felt her legs shift, her arms twitch, but they would do no more than this. She tried over and over and over again, and soon it was bringing on a dull pain that grew with each attempt.

She saw movement to her right and managed to loll her head in that direction. Gods, a *mound* of irindai were rising, pulling away from their brethren. It was vaguely man-shaped, she realized.

Or *boy*-shaped.

As the form came forth, the moths began fluttering away, returning to their previous positions, and a second form began to emerge. Whole flocks of moths peeled away, revealing two boys with dark skin and bright blue eyes, and one of them, Hidi, with that terrible scar running down his cheek.

Hidi glanced to the archway where Rümayesh had recently gone. Makuo came straight for Çeda, a gentle smile on his lips. "You are here," he said in a Kundhunese accent so thick Çeda could barely understand him.

"Yuh . . ." Çeda licked her lips and tried again. "You wuh-wanted me here."

Hidi came and stood next to Makuo. "Yes, and now you come."

"Buh . . . But I commanded you. Ashwandi . . ."

"Yes," said Makuo, "and we are bound. We listened."

53

"I s-said . . . to release me."

Hidi tilted his head, as if speaking to a child. "And we will obey. We will give you the keys."

"What do you mean?"

"You must release yourself," said Hidi in a sharp tone. "Rümayesh is not so easy to move as that."

"H-how?"

Hidi ignored her, choosing to step around the perimeter of the cellar, while Makuo reached into Çeda's black thawb and pulled out her mother's locket.

"Luh-leave that alone!"

"Calm yourself, girl." He pried it open, revealing the two petals Çeda had placed inside. She'd normally have nothing inside, or perhaps one if she was expecting trouble, but she'd started carrying two for the fear that was constantly running through her.

Makuo took them, then whistled two sharp notes. A flurry of cressetwings descended from the ceiling, one of them alighting on Makuo's outstretched finger, the rest continuing to fly around and above his head. With care, Makuo set the two petals onto the wings of the moth. The petals remained there, as if they'd been a part of the moth from the moment it struggled free of its chrysalis. Makuo whistled again, and the moth on his finger flew to rejoin the swarm.

Bit by bit, they retook their positions, but in doing so Çeda completely lost the one with the petals. She searched frantically, but couldn't find it. "Where is it?"

At this the boys smiled and spoke in unison, "And what fun we going have if we be giving you that?" They glanced to the archway, and Hidi began backing away. Moths flew toward him, landing on him, layering his form as if consuming him. "You got to play the *game*, girl," Hidi said as he was swallowed whole.

"Look to the flames." Makuo touched his hand to Çeda's cheek, then he too began backing away, following his brother. "Look to the flames and you'll find it sure."

Soon both of them had been consumed by the irindai, and all was still. She could hear her own heartbeat, so complete was the silence.

She looked among the irindai, from one to the next to the next, trying to find the one with the petals, but it was so bloody dim she couldn't tell if one merely had a brighter mark of flame than usual or if it was indeed the one she needed.

While she searched, she worked her muscles—her legs, her arms, her neck, her torso. She thought the pain would ebb, but it only seemed to grow worse the more she moved. Gritting her teeth, she managed to bend her limbs, to regain some sense of normal movement, even if it was slow, even if it felt as though her muscles were made of bright, molten metal.

Just when she was ready to sit up, she heard the door opening, and this time many sets of footsteps approached. Kadir came first, but others followed, men and women dressed in white thawbs or full-length kaftans, and with them came the reek of the sort of tabbaq that would make one high. Some wore niqabs or veiled turbans to hide their faces, but most were unadorned, and came holding flutes of golden wine or stubby glasses filled with araq. Others held nothing at all, preferring to cross their arms or hold them behind their backs as they stared at the irindai or Rümayesh or Çeda.

In her desperation, Çeda tried to lift herself from the cold slab upon which she lay, but before she could do more than curl her head and shoulders up off the slab, Kadir came rushing to her side and pressed her back down. Those gathered watched with jackal eyes, hyena grins, as Kadir leaned in. "Stay where you are until spoken to," he whispered, "and perhaps you'll leave this place whole." Unlike Rümayesh, who was soft velvet, a knife in the dark, Kadir was a cold, bloody hammer, every bit as blunt and every bit as deadly.

She grit her teeth and stared up, not wanting to give Kadir the satisfaction of seeing the fear in her eyes, and that was when she noticed it. Makuo's irindai, slowly fanning its wings almost directly overhead. How could she have missed it earlier? And now that she *had* seen it, it was like a bloody great beacon. A fire on the horizon.

With care, praying Kadir wouldn't notice, she averted her gaze, lay still, and tried to quell her rapid breathing. Kadir did glance up, momentary confusion contorting his features. Eventually he retreated to one corner of the room, and relief flooded through Çeda.

From a pedestal Kadir picked up a heavy bronze cymbal and a leather-wrapped rod made from the same metal. He ran the rod around the cymbal's edge, creating a strangely hypnotic sound. The irindai responded immediately, their wings moving at a slower pace in time to the rhythm of the cymbal.

"The preliminaries are over," Rümayesh said. "I trust you'll enjoy what I've found for you, a rare little bird indeed. A Sharakhani through and through, with mystery upon mystery we can unravel together. Please"—she motioned around her to the walls, to the low ceiling— "choose, and our young maid will follow."

Those gathered began walking about the room, looking up to the ceiling, plucking a single moth from the writhing mass. Çeda tried as well as she could not to stare at the moth with the adichara petals, but she was so worried that someone would take it that she found her eyes flicking there every so often. One of the women noticed.

Eyes glazed, she stared up at the ceiling where Çeda's gaze had wandered. Her hand wavered near Çeda's cressetwing, but the gods must have been watching over Çeda, for the woman chose another less than a hand's-breadth away.

One by one, those gathered opened their mouths and placed the moth within, taking great care to prevent harm to the delicate wings. Without exception, their eyes flickered closed as soon as the irindai was taken within them. Their eyelids opened and closed like the wings of the irindai, then they stood still, watching Çeda or Rümayesh or one another in a half-lidded daze.

Rümayesh strode to Çeda's side.

"Choose," was all she said.

Çeda stared defiantly, as if she were conflicted, as if she might very well do something desperate at any moment. She would take the cressetwing the boys meant for her but, when she did so, she wanted Rümayesh's eyes on *her* and nowhere else. With care, Çeda stood. She felt strangely alone with Rümayesh, even with so many of those gathered staring dazedly at the two of them. With as much speed as she could manage, she grabbed the cressetwing with the petals and stuffed it into her mouth.

She had planned to chew it immediately, to devour it, but the moment the moth's delicate wings touched her tongue, a euphoric rush welled up from somewhere deep inside. It brought with it an endless flow of thoughts and memories, their combined fabric flickering like the surface of a sun-dappled river.

Her mother raising her wooden shinai in the air, waiting for Çeda to do the same.

Running through the dusty streets of Sharakhai with Emre, each with a mound of stolen pistachios cradled in their arms, shells dripping like rain as they sprint along.

Peeking through the parted blankets of a stall in the spice market late at night as Havasham, the handsome son of Athel the carpetmonger, thrusts himself over and over between the legs of Lina, a girl three years Çeda's elder who is not beautiful but has a way of talking with the boys with that sharp tongue of hers that makes them want her.

Çeda felt her consciousness attempt to expand, to encompass all of who she was, all she'd experienced. She wondered, even as her own awareness threatened to consume her, whether everyone experienced this same thing or if it was to do with the petals. She could feel it now— the verve the petals granted her, the strength, the awareness.

Through the irindai she could feel others' minds as well: those closest, their eagerness to feel more from Çeda; those beyond, who had done this many times before but because of that hungered to experience it again; and Rümayesh, who was someone different altogether.

Where Rümayesh stood, there were two, not one.

Two minds, sharing the same body. One, a lady of Sharakhai, highborn, a woman who'd lived in her estate in Goldenhill her entire life.

And the other—

A chill rushed down Çeda's frame as more memories tumbled past.

Cutting her first purse, the exhilaration as she ran down the Trough, the lanky man chasing after her.

Swimming naked in the Haddah in spring with Emre and Tariq and Hamid, feeling the small fishes nip at her ankles and toes.

She drew herself in, ignoring the rush of her life, focusing instead on the second soul inside the woman who stood before her. It was something Çeda had never seen or experienced before. How could she have? Its mind was deep, foreign, and by the gods *old*—not in the way Ibrahim the storyteller was old, nor even in the way the Kings of Sharakhai, who'd seen the passage of four centuries, were old, but in the way the city was old. In the way the desert was old.

This was no human, but some creature of the desert, some vestige of the desert's making, or one of the ehrekh that haunted the forgotten corners of the Great Shangazi.

Çeda knew immediately that few others had ever felt this being's presence, for it now awoke from a slumber of sorts. It grew fearful, if only for the span of a heartbeat, and in the wake of that realization, Rümayesh—or the woman Çeda had *thought* was Rümayesh—strode forward and placed her hand around Çeda's neck, gripping it tightly enough to limit Çeda's breath. She leaned down and stared into Çeda's eyes, imposing her will, sifting through Çeda's memories.

Çeda couldn't allow this.

She couldn't allow Rümayesh to have her way, for if she did, she would be forever lost.

This was the gift of the adichara petals that Hidi and Makuo had granted her—the ability to remain above the effects of the irindai, at least to some small degree.

But what to do about Rümayesh?

As more memories were examined, then tossed aside like uncut jewels, Çeda thought desperately for something that might divide these two, something that might give the highborn woman a reason to throw off the chains Rümayesh had placed on her.

She found it moments later. A memory flashed past—of stepping into the blooming fields to cut one of the adichara flowers. It was discarded immediately by Rümayesh, but the woman huddling beneath that greater consciousness, a highborn woman of Sharakhai, flared in anger and indignation. Rümayesh tried to settle on Çeda's first fight in the pits, but Çeda drew her mind back to the twisted trees that grew in a vast ring outside the city's limits. Had Çeda not had the effects of the adichara running through her, she would surely have succumbed to the onslaught Rümayesh threw against her defenses. But with the petals she was able to focus on that memory, to share it with all those gathered within the cellar.

Çeda pads along the sand as the twin moons shine brightly above. The adichara's thorned branches sway, limned in moonlight. They click and clack and creak, a symphony of movement in the otherwise-still air. Çeda looks among the blooms, which glow softly in the moonlight, a river of stars over an endless sea. She chooses not the widest, nor the brightest, but the bloom that seems to be facing the moons unshrinkingly, then cuts it with a swift stroke of her kenshar, tucking away the cutting in a pouch at her belt.

Çeda had expected anger from the woman Rümayesh controlled. What she hadn't expected was anger from the others gathered here. She should have, though. They would have the blood of Kings running through their veins; they would know every bit as well as Çeda the sort of crime they were witnessing. A woman stealing into the blooming fields to take of the adichara insulted not only the Kings but all who revered the twisted trees.

They began to mumble and murmur, more and more of their number waking from the dream they shared. At first they stepped forward like boneyard shamblers, but with every moment that passed they seemed to come more alive.

Behind them, the highborn woman Rümayesh controlled railed against her bonds. She was more angry, more aware of herself, than she'd been in years, and she was buoyed by the anger of those around her. Rümayesh's will was still strong, however. She held against the assault, the two of them at a stalemate. Soon, though, the woman's anger began to ebb. Before long, Rümayesh would regain the control she'd had over this woman.

Çeda had lost track of those around her. She realized with a start that one of the men was holding a kenshar. A woman on Çeda's opposite side drew a slim knife of her own. A remnant of Çeda's earlier lethargy still remained, but fear now drove her. She rolled backward, coming to a crouch, waiting for any to approach.

A moment later the man did, the woman right after, but they both gave clumsy swipes of their blades. Çeda leapt over the man, snaking her arm around his neck as she went. She landed and levered him so that he tipped backward, then controlled him, moving him slowly toward the door.

He tried to use his knife to strike at her arm, but she was ready. She released his neck at the last moment and snatched the wrist holding the knife with one hand, closed her other hand around his fist, the one wrapped around the weapon. Then she drew his own knife toward his neck. He was so surprised he hardly fought her, and by the time he realized what was happening, it was too late. The knife slipped into his throat like a needle through ripe summer fruit. For a moment, everyone stared at the blood coursing down over Çeda's hands and arms. No one moved. Their eyes began to roll up in their heads. They were not only *witnessing* his death, Çeda realized; they *felt* it through their shared bond.

As the man's heart slowed and finally stopped, the irindai burst from the walls and from the ceiling. The air became thick with them, fluttering, touching skin, making eyes bat, becoming caught in hair.

Çeda's mind burned in the thoughts and emotions of all those gathered. They were of one mind, now, sharing what they'd known, what they hoped to be, what they feared in the deepest recesses of their minds. It was too much, a flood that consumed them all, one by one.

Çeda screamed, a single note added to the cacophony of screams filling this small space, then fell beneath the weight of their collected dreams.

Çeda opened her eyes, finding a dark-skinned boy with bright blue eyes staring at her.

"The sun shining bright, girl," Makuo said. "Time you return to it. Let it see your face before it forget."

"What?" Çeda sat up slowly, her mind still lost in the land of dreams. She remembered who she was now—her name, her purpose here—but it seemed like an age and a day since she'd fallen to the weight of the minds around her.

Across the floor of the cellar, bodies lay everywhere like leaves tossed by the wind. Layer upon layer of dead moths covered their forms. Hidi stood by a sarcophagus, staring into its depths. It was what Çeda had been lying upon, she realized. The lid had been removed and now lay cracked and broken to one side.

Çeda stood and took one step toward the sarcophagus, but Makuo stopped her. "This isn't for you," the boy said.

Within the sarcophagus, she saw the crown of a head, wiry black hair, two twisted horns sweeping back from the forehead.

She thought of pressing Makuo. The two of them had won, she knew. They'd beaten Rümayesh with Çeda's help, and until now they'd considered her their ally, but that could change at any moment.

Steer you well wide of the will of the gods, old Ibrahim had always said after finishing one of his tragic stories. She'd heard dozens of those stories, and none of them ended happily. She'd always thought it a trick of Ibrahim's storytelling, to end them so, but now she wasn't so sure.

"What of Ashwandi?" Çeda asked.

Hidi looked up from whatever it was that had him transfixed, his scar puckering as he bared his teeth. "She free now. Her sister's wish was always for Ashwandi to leave the ehrekh's side, to return to the grasslands."

An ehrekh, then . . .

Rümayesh was an ehrekh, a twisted yet powerful experiment of the god Goezhen. Few ehrekh remained in the desert, but those that did were powerful indeed.

"Is she alive?"

"Oh, yes," the boys said in unison, their eyes full of glee, "she lives."

"What will you do with her?" Çeda asked, tilting her head toward the sarcophagus.

At this they frowned. Hidi returned his gaze to Rümayesh's sleeping form, while Makuo took Çeda by the shoulders and led her away. "The sun shining bright," he said. "Time you return to it."

Çeda let herself be led from the cellar, but her tread was heavy. Rümayesh may have tricked Çeda, may have wanted to steal her memories, but something didn't feel right about leaving her to these godling boys.

Makuo led her up a set of winding stairs and at last to

a metal door. Çeda paused, her hand resting above the handle.

Steer you well wide of the will of the gods.

There was wisdom in those words, she thought as she gripped the door's warm handle. Surely there was wisdom. Then she opened the door and stepped into the sunlight.

Part Two

Born of a Trickster God

A T THE EDGE OF SHARAKHAI'S GRAND BAZAAR, a crowd had gathered beneath the old fig tree. Çeda could *hear* the man she'd come to see, old Ibrahim the storyteller, but she couldn't yet see him. The sheer density of the gathering wouldn't allow it from her current vantage, so she skirted the crowd, standing tiptoes every so often and looking for an opening.

As she walked, the desert wind toyed with the fig tree's branches. The movement gave life to the sunlight, stippling the assemblage with pinpricks of light. Men, women, and children, burnooses and kaftans and abayas, brightened then darkened, making them seem to sway, first this way, then that. It was a riot of color and movement that became so dreamlike Çeda had to blink and look away until she'd recovered.

Ibrahim was one of the city's most popular storytellers, but even so this crowd was unusually large. Çeda had no idea why at first, but then she vaguely recalled Seyhan the spice merchant mentioning the caravans when she'd stopped by his stall the day before. More than a dozen of them—two hundred ships all told—were setting sail over the desert tomorrow. For many who'd come to Sharakhai, the siren call of the city was strong. They wanted one last chance to wander the stalls of the bazaar, to pick up a bag or two from the spice market, to hear a tale from the exotic city they'd so longed to visit. And so, even though it was the time of day when Ibrahim would normally have returned home to grab a bite to eat and have a short nap while the desert's warmest hours sailed past, the storyteller had remained. Ibrahim, like most in Shara-khai, would suffer much for money.

When she made it past the row of fruit sellers, a space opened up and she saw Ibrahim clearly at last. He was spreading his arms theatrically as he wove his tale, his baritone rasp waxing gaily about the goddess Nalamae and her travels across the Great Shangazi. His old, dusty blanket was spread on the ground, coins glinting on its surface like bright cities on a map of the Five Kingdoms. Again the play of light, this time on the coins, made her feel as though the ground beneath her was unsteady. She breathed deeply, pinching the inner corners of her eyes, though it did little to clear the burning itch of lost sleep.

When she opened her eyes again, she tried to focus only on Ibrahim. He was just telling the crowd how Nalamae, after giving life to the River Haddah, had wandered the desert, creating oases that the twelve tribes could use in their ceaseless wanderings. He had his wide-brimmed hat off and was using it to fan himself, though when he came to a particularly dramatic moment he'd slip it back on his head and spread his arms in broad sweeps. Every so often, someone in the audience would toss a copper or a few six-pieces at the storyteller's feet; one even dropped two sylval before walking away, those nearby shifting like soldiers to fill the gap.

Ibrahim's voice, the rapt audience, the bright sun, a tableau that likened itself to a dream. The occasional clink of coins would momentarily pull her from the trance, but then the dream would resume and whisper in her ear to lie at the foot of the tree and curl up in sleep.

"Are you very well?" a low voice rumbled.

Çeda nearly jumped from her skin. She turned and saw a man with dark skin, wearing a rich ivory tunic and toga, staring at her with a look of mild concern. The more she stared at him, saying nothing, the more his concern deepened.

"You need something to drink, girl?"

It was more statement than question, and perhaps she did, but before she could reply, a cup was being pressed into her hand. Rosewater lemonade, laced with peppercorn and nutmeg. She drank deeply from it, then reached into the purse at her belt for a copper khet to give the man, but he took her hand in both of his, keeping the coin where it lay in the palm of her hand.

"Keep it and be well."

"Thank you."

The man was soon lost among the ceaselessly shifting traffic of the bazaar. Somehow by the time she'd finished the lemonade and returned her attention toward Ibrahim, the crowd was breaking up. Ibrahim himself had already collected his coins from the blanket and was walking away. She sprinted to catch up, blinking the sleep away, and fell into step alongside him.

"There you are," Ibrahim said as he took off his hat, ran a sleeve over his sweating brow, and replaced it. The brim bounced as they walked toward the Spear, one of the busiest thoroughfares in Sharakhai. "What's happened to you?"

"Nothing." She drew in a sharp breath. "What do you mean?"

"Are you having trouble with Emre? Is he treating you well?"

"What? Of course he is!"

"Well there's *something* the matter. You look like my mule's been treading on you for days, girl."

Çeda tried to keep herself from blinking, but she became so conscious of it she was forced to pinch the bridge of her nose and clamp her eyes shut for a bit of relief. "I haven't been sleeping well."

"Do tell . . . The question is, why not?"

"Are we trading, Ibrahim?"

He considered her for a moment. "If there's something you wish from me, then yes, I'll trade for this."

She had meant it as a joke, but she could see that Ibrahim was serious. "I don't know if I'm willing to trade it," she said.

She was used to Ibrahim's affable nature, his easy laugh, so when he stopped just short of the Spear and turned to face her with the most serious look she'd ever seen on him, she was caught off-guard. His kindly old eyes looked her up and down as the sounds of traffic passed along the Spear behind him. "I've never seen you like this, Çeda. You're normally the bright star, but the girl I see before me is nothing more than a guttering candle."

A blade glowing red from the heat of a fire, the edge moving ever closer. Çeda blinked away the image. "As I said, I haven't been sleeping well."

"Then tell me why. Ibrahim might be able to help."

"In all our dealings, Ibrahim, you have made me tell my stories first. This time, you'll tell me what *I* wish to know, and *then* I'll tell you something in return."

Ever the businessman was Ibrahim, so much so that she thought he might deny her request, but he didn't. "Very well." He resumed walking, guiding Çeda to the right when they reached the Spear and merged into the jostling traffic. "Ask me your questions."

"I wish to know of the ehrekh," Çeda said softly so those around them would have difficulty overhearing.

"What of them?"

"Can they be imprisoned?"

Ibrahim shrugged. "There are many stories of magi imprisoning ehrekh, though most close with a dramatic and unfortunate end for the ones who had the impressively bad idea to do so."

"How? How can they be imprisoned?"

"Most tales tell of the magi learning their true names."

"But then what?" Çeda asked. "They are bound to your word if you but speak their name?"

As they stepped around a dray plodding its way forward against the flow, Ibrahim couldn't hide the momentary knitting of his brow. "No, Çeda, I don't believe knowledge of a name is sufficient. There are dark rituals that surround the summoning of an ehrekh, and they all deal in blood. Liberally."

"Can the ehrekh die?" Çeda asked as the crowd shouted at the driver of the dray to move to the far side of the street, where the flow was heading west.

"There are stories of their deaths, yes, though most of these have been at the hands of the gods when the ehrekh stood in their way."

"How? How can they be killed?"

"Now *there's* a question. Why do you wish to know, Çeda?"

"I'm not ready to tell my story yet."

Ibrahim considered her, then waved them on, into the path of five young men carrying patterned yellow carpets over their shoulders. "They can fall to the blade. They can fall to fire. They can fall to the will of the gods. But they do none of these things easily. They are cruel, wicked beasts that love to toy with us, with the tribes and others who stumble across their homes in the corners of the Great Shangazi."

"And do they have souls?"

"As you and I have souls?"

Çeda shrugged. "I guess so."

Ibrahim paused. "Shall I tell you a tale, Çeda?"

"Will it cost me?"

He laughed. "No more than you had already planned to give."

"Very well," Çeda said cautiously.

"You know that Goezhen the Wicked created the ehrekh."

She nodded.

"Well, it is said that he did so while Tulathan was imprisoned by Yerinde. You know the tale?"

She nodded again. Ages ago, Yerinde, a winsome goddess taken by fits of passion, had stolen the moon goddess away. *For love,* she had professed when Tulathan had eventually been freed by her sister, Rhia. *It was always for love.*

"Goezhen stole into Yerinde's mountain fastness," Ibrahim went on, "and there he found Tulathan hidden deep underground in a lightless oubliette. Tulathan begged him to free her, but Goezhen refused, and stole her tears when she wept for her lost freedom. He went to Rhia then, and told her the tale of her lost sister. Rhia raged, and Goezhen stole her screams. The gods didn't know why Goezhen had done these things, but they found out much later that when he left Yerinde's tower and returned to the desert, he made the first of the eh-rekh. He gave them Tulathan's tears that they might have blood. He gave them Rhia's cries that they might have voice. They are rage-filled things, Çeda, and not to be trifled with. And that is all I will say on the subject. Now tell me why you've come to me with haunted eyes, asking of the twisted creations of the god of chaos."

Çeda considered as the roar of the Wheel at the city's center rose up around them. Thousands were leading wagons and horses and mules and children around it, moving from this part of the city to that. Çeda and Ibrahim flowed with traffic and headed south along the Trough. Çeda might have spoken in the anonymity of that roar, but she waited until the tumult had settled before speaking once more. "There are ehrekh hidden within the walls of the city, did you know?"

"I've heard whispers," Ibrahim said.

"One has been known to whisk unfortunate souls away to some hidden place and sift through their memories like so much sand. It holds these memories up for others to witness, to relive as if they were their own."

Ibrahim's sweaty brow furrowed, and his eyes grew instantly worried. "Rümayesh," he breathed.

Çeda nodded. "But the ehrekh are not so powerful that they can't become victims themselves. There are those who might take them, hide *them* away."

"Çeda—"

"And if that were to happen, the ehrekh might reach out, speak to one through her dreams."

"Çeda, *who*? Who has done this?"

Çeda stopped and looked up to Ibrahim, traffic parting and passing around them like storm-blown sand. Gods, how she wanted to tell him. He might well be able to help her if she let him. But it was so much bigger than the two of them, and dangerous besides. It had nearly killed her once already, and a man like Ibrahim, a man who'd always been kind to her, didn't deserve to get drawn into it. "It's only a story I've heard."

She turned and walked the other away, back along the Trough, but called over her shoulder, "Fair payment for what you've given me."

———

It was sunset by the time Çeda reached her home in Roseridge. A fragrant braiding of floral scents drifted down as she took the stairs up from ground level. She knew the scents well: ashwagandha and passionflower and schisandra. She ought to. They'd been her constant companions this past month, when she'd finally given in and begun steeping an elixir she'd hoped would quell the dreams that plagued her.

When she opened the door, she found Emre kneeling on the carpet before the small oven in the center of the room. A pot sat atop it. Emre stirred the contents methodically, all but ignoring Çeda.

Bless you, Emre. The scent was so strong she nearly closed her eyes and fell asleep standing. "You didn't need to do this," she said as she closed the door behind her.

Emre, his dark eyes looking up to her with concern, tapped the wooden spoon against the lip of the pot, then laid it across the top. "It's almost ready." He stood and wiped his hands self-consciously, eyeing Çeda. "And yes, I did. You've looked like death himself this past month."

"You've looked like a horse's ass your whole life, but you don't see me making any elixirs for *that*." Weeks ago he might have laughed, but today he stared at her with an uncomfortable expression. *Gods, he's truly worried.* "It's going to be all right," she said. "It's only a few nightmares."

"At first, maybe. Then it was just a shout in the night. Then it was blood-curdling cries. But last night, Çeda, you screamed and screamed, even *after* I woke you." His eyes narrowed. "You don't even remember, do you?"

A knife's edge gleaming, coming ever closer. The smell of burnt flesh. "I remember the dreams."

"Because you're fully in their grip."

He'd said as much before, that she'd been captured somehow. He was asking her without words—after his endless queries had gotten him nowhere—what had happened those months ago. She'd never told him of the eh-rekh, Rümayesh, of her time with that ancient creature who had managed to hide herself among the warp and weft of life in Sharakhai. It had felt like a dream. It still did. She'd thought it a memory that would pass. But then the nightmares had come, and she'd lost sleep. They'd remained, and she'd begun mixing an elixir to help shake them. And now Emre was brewing them so she wouldn't have to. What was next? Would he be spooning it to her while she babbled in her bed like old Ghiza across the way?

"It's ready," Çeda said, nodding to the simmering pot.

"What *happened*, Çeda?"

"They're only dreams."

"And they started days after you'd gone missing. Quite the coincidence, don't you think?"

She couldn't really say why she wanted that experience to remain a mystery to Emre. Perhaps because she'd been so helpless, subject to Rümayesh's every whim. Or perhaps because she'd come so close to dying. Or perhaps because the godling children, Makuo and Hidi, had made her fear to come near them again. It was all of those things to some degree, but she knew the primary reason she was hiding it was because she was embarrassed to admit it all to Emre. She knew it wasn't so, but it felt like a thing she had done to herself. *And there's nothing you can get yourself into,* her mother used to tell her, *that you can't get yourself out of as well.*

"You've made a good batch." She motioned to the pot, breathing in its scent. "I can tell."

He stared at her, clearly struggling with just how hard he should push her, but then he let out a breath and shrugged. "I ought to. I've watched you make dozens of them."

"Let's try it then." She winked. "See just what sort of apothecary you'd make."

He sneered at her, then shook his head and fetched an earthenware mug and used a small piece of cheesecloth to sieve the solids from the pot and allow the bright red liquid to filter into the mug. It steamed as he handed it to her.

She leaned in and kissed him on the cheek. "Thank you."

She collapsed into bed immediately after finishing the draught.

———

Far into the desert, well beyond the borders of Sharakhai, a woman lies on a bed of stone.

The sound of skittering comes. Of stone shifting.

To her right, an open window yawns. A cold morning breeze steals into the room, the smell it carries like the cooling of the world after its making. The woman rolls her head toward the window and sees through it a steep ridge with rank after rank of trees standing sentinel along it. The trees are strange, though. They have no boughs, no branches, for they were turned to stone on the day of her making in this, the very place of her birth.

Even the simple effort of turning her head is painful, so she turns away from the window until she stares once more at the stone ceiling and the ghastly light now splashed across its skin. Its surface reads like a map, charting her life over the course of aeons in the desert. She sees within its topography her awakening when Goezhen himself placed his lips to hers and granted her her first breath. She sees in it her wanderings after her birth, years untold in which she trekked along the vast mountain ranges that ring the Great Shangazi. It is a circuit she completed seven times in order to assimilate within her very soul the borders of the desert and all that lay within. She sees in the stone her first steps as she returns to the endless sands, the first time she'd ever disguised herself. She posed as a lost traveler and sailed with the desert tribes for generations, often moving from tribe to tribe.

An amberlark calls in the distance, little more than a gentle cooing, but to her it sounds like the screams of the women and men she lured away from their brothers and sisters into the desert deep, where she picked them apart, bit by bit, to see what they were made of. These are ancient memories of days she'd nearly forgotten, days that brought her no particular pride, but no particular sense of shame, either. She was inexperienced then, and curious about these humans that Goezhen seemed both to love and to hate. How many souls has she toyed with in the ages spent wandering the desert?

Many . . .

The sounds of footsteps approach.

Many, indeed.

In the corner, a dull red flame ignites like a beacon fire.

And now the sands have turned.

"She's awake," came a voice in the darkness, speaking the rolling tongue of the Kundhunese.

"I feel her," replies the one near the brazier.

The glowing coals outline his form in ruddy light. He looks like one of the first gods working with the protean stuff of the stars to forge a new world. It's probably how he views himself, though he and his brother are nothing more than a twinkling of Onondu's eye—childling gods come to torment another childling god.

We are cousins of a sort, we three. The thought makes her smile. *Isn't pain dealt by family the deepest pain of all?*

From the darkness, a form approaches. "Are you ready?" Makuo says.

She says nothing in return.

"I know it mean much to you," he says in stilted Sharakhan, "but what is that compared to what we do to you? What we *will* do to you?" He reaches her side. The pale morning light casts his eyes an icy blue. His dark skin looks sickly.

Her voice is an ancient door opening. "This is senseless." Despite the ages she's lived, despite all she has done and might yet do, there is fear in her heart for the pain that is coming. The boys are gifted in this if nothing else.

"I've told you. I don't *know* where it is." It is the truth, but she sees the disbelief in Makuo's eyes. She sees that he will *never* believe her.

From her prone vantage his arm distends strangely, his hand reaching toward her. As his fingers brush her cheek, she feels herself falling away, down, down, deep as she's ever gone. Away from the light. Away from the touch of Makuo's fingers. Away from the pain.

"She trying hide again," Hidi says by the brazier.

"I know," Makuo says as he stares into her eyes, trying to prevent her departure, "but she cannot escape the pain. Some will still reach her."

Hidi steps away from the brazier, a curved knife held in one hand. The blade glows dully. The edge gleams a violent red. As he reaches her side, he speaks to her in Sharakhan, as if speaking the tongue she'd adopted these past many centuries would endear him to her. "Tell me now. Tell me where you hide it, and we will end this river of pain."

But she is well into her hidden place now. His form is dimming. She can barely hear his words. She can see the knife, though, wavering before her like a battering ram, a mouth aflame, set to raze the walls she'd built brick by painstaking brick.

"No?" Hidi asked. Then he shrugs. "Soon or late, you will come see things as we do."

The blade lowers. She feels Hidi's cold hand on her ankle, just above where the cold iron shackle bites into her skin.

A searing pain enters her body just above it. *"Kadir!"*

Hidi laughs, his eyes now filled with glee. "Your man long gone. Him think you dead. But *I* am here. My *brother* here."

The pain broadens, tearing at her world until it is all that is left. *"Kadir!"*

———

Çeda's eyes shot open. Her body was rigid as a spear, shuddering from the white hot pain in her right leg. "Kadir!" She thrashed, trying to throw off whoever or whatever was holding her.

"Çeda, it's me!"

She stared wildly around the small room with the plastered mudbrick walls. It was Makuo, standing over her.

Or Hidi, with that cruel scar on his cheek.

"Çeda, you're dreaming again!"

She blinked.

Hidi's face faded, and she recognized Emre at last. He hovered over her, his hands clamped against her arms, pressing her down.

The glowing blade. The searing pain as it drove into her

legs, into her ankles and knees, through the walls of the tower she'd so carefully constructed.

Her nightdress was drenched in sweat. The breeze blowing through the windows was chill. She shivered horribly, from the memories, perhaps, or the sleepless nights, or the directionless fear that now surrounded her.

Emre's eyes took her in, assessing her. When he was sure she'd fully risen from her dream he released her and reached for the mug on the bedside table. Emre, bless him, had refilled it. Steam, lit silver by the moonlight, rose from the elixir, twisting and drifting before vanishing altogether. Çeda could smell its complex bouquet of floral scents, which somehow did more to ground her to this place and this time than Emre's shouting.

"I can't go back to sleep, Emre. Not tonight." She pulled herself up in her bed and propped herself against the wall behind her. "Some proper tea instead? I feel so very dry."

He looked ready to argue, but when he stared into her eyes, he must have seen something that convinced him she wouldn't fall back to sleep, for he visibly deflated and set the mug down. "Of course, just wait here." He left the room and returned a short while later with tea. As she held the hot mug and breathed in the loamy scent, Emre scraped the nearby chair over and sat down. "Blood of the gods, what's *happening*, Çeda?"

"I . . . It's hard to explain."

"Try. Please. Because this can't go on."

She nodded, sipping gratefully from the honey-laced tea. She didn't want to lay her troubles at Emre's feet—this was *her* problem to solve—but she admitted the mere thought of someone else, *anyone* else, knowing the story would be a huge relief. "Two months ago," she finally said, "after the fight with Brama, I was abducted by an ehrekh."

Emre's eyes narrowed and a smile tugged the corners of his lips as if he suspected a joke, but then his face grew intensely serious. "You were?"

"Her name is Rümayesh, and she became . . . interested in me. She tried to take my memories from me using irindai, cressetwing moths, but before she could, two godling children came and took *her*." Çeda wanted to laugh at how ridiculous it all sounded. "*Where* they took her, I don't know, but her dreams have haunted me ever since."

When she closed her eyes, she could still see Hidi's dark silhouette against the backdrop of the glowing brazier.

"But why?" Emre asked.

She blinked, banishing the memory. "I think she's pleading for me to help."

"*Help?* Why would she ask for help from you?"

"Perhaps there's no one else to ask. Hidi and Makuo are children of Onondu. I knew little enough about them then, but I've made a point of reading more since. Onondu is a wrathful god, very powerful in his homeland, Kundhun, powerful enough that it's not unreasonable to believe that two of his children would come all this way to subdue the likes of Rümayesh, even as powerful as she is."

"Gods, Çeda, what have you gotten yourself into?"

She tried to smile but felt only fear for the next time she would fall asleep and dream those terrible dreams.

Emre's eyes had gone distant. "Maybe you should leave."

"What? Sharakhai?" She wanted to laugh. "And where would I go?"

He focused on her once more. "Who cares as long as it keeps you alive?"

"Who's to say she wouldn't try harder? Who's to say I could *ever* escape those dreams? I might travel the world and never be free of them. At least in Sharakhai I have friends."

"And a fat lot of good *we're* doing you."

She sipped at her tea. "It helps, Emre. All of it helps."

"Who is Kadir?"

Çeda felt as though she'd been shot through the heart.

By the gods, she thought, *the way Rümayesh had screamed his name . . .*

"Çeda, why are you looking at me like that?"

She forced herself to focus on Emre. "Kadir is her servant, a vizir of sorts. In my dreams, Rümayesh calls his name, and I *thought* she was calling him for help even though she knew Kadir couldn't hear her. I thought it was a reaction to the pain." She ran her fingers through her unkempt hair. "I can't believe I never thought of it before."

"Thought of *what*?"

"Calling his name. It was a message. To *me*. All this time I thought Rümayesh wasn't aware of the bond we share, our connection through my dreams, but I realize now she's been trying to send me a message all along."

Emre's eyes narrowed. "But if that were true, she could have told you straight away."

"I'm not so sure. It only seems to happen when Hidi and Makuo come for her, and while they torture her. Maybe their presence, or her fear, is what allows her to reach me, but with them so close she can't speak plainly."

"That feels flimsy as eggshells, Çeda."

"No. I need to find Kadir, Emre. There's nothing else for me to do. And if it turns out I'm wrong, if he knows nothing, then I'm no worse off than I am now."

"Is he a threat to you?"

Çeda shrugged. "Without Rümayesh, I don't think so. And if I help him to find her, I imagine he'll feel indebted."

"You want to help him *find* her? A creature who preyed upon you? A creature who was ready to cast your secrets about the city like seeds?"

"I don't know what else to do." She felt miserable and was sure she looked worse, but at least she had some small hope now.

Emre stood. He looked as though he'd forgotten something and was on the cusp of remembering what it was. "How much money do you have?"

"What, here?"

"Everything, Çeda."

"Why?"

"Just tell me."

"Maybe twenty rahl, all told."

His eyes went hard. "There's a man I know who might help."

"Who?"

A strange look crossed Emre's features, as if he were worried. "A man named Adzin, but I don't know if he'll even see us." He left her room through the beaded curtains across her door.

"Emre, who is he?"

"Just rest!" Their entry door opened. "Have more tea,

then get the money together!" The door closed, and she heard his footsteps clomping in a rush down toward the street.

Late that evening as the sun was setting, Emre led Çeda to Sharakhai's sandy western harbor. Walking along the misshapen arc of the quay, they eventually came to a tumbledown pier, where an old sloop was moored.

"This is where we're to meet him," Emre said.

Çeda pointed at the ship. "Here? It looks like the Silver Spears beat it and left it for dead."

"It's just for appearances," Emre replied, though his voice was far from confident. "He doesn't want to attract undue attention. You of all people should understand that."

"Well, it seems to attract termites well enough," she said under her breath. "Will it even sail?"

"Let's hope so," he said, and proceeded down the pier, stopping just short of stepping across the narrow gap between ship and pier and onto the deck of the sandship. Çeda followed, watching as a towering Kundhunese deckhand moved about the ship with a lantern, golden light reflecting eerily off his black skin. Three other crewmen climbed along the rigging, preparing the sails and tidying a ship that looked as patchwork as patchwork could be.

"We're here for Adzin," Emre said.

The hulking Kundhuni lifted his lantern and shone it, first on Emre, then Çeda. He seemed ill-pleased, but in the end he grunted, swung the lantern toward the open hatch near the gangway, and walked away. As the lantern cast ghostly patterns against the masts and rigging, Emre motioned for Çeda to go ahead of him. After stepping onto the ship and crossing the deck, she took an angled ladder down to a passageway that made her shiver just to look at it.

Its walls and ceiling were lined with hooks, and from these, strings were looped like the weave of some madman. Tied to the strings were an assortment of ornaments and oddments that were dark-stained, feculent, misused, as though each had been plucked from the grip of a freshly dead hand: a bent awl, its aged wooden handle cracked; a misshapen pair of wrought iron scissors; a tarnished silver ring with a setting filled with what appeared to be children's teeth; a string of—dear gods, were those *fingernails?*—hung loosely around the neck of a wooden doll with the face of a little boy painted on it. Çeda hadn't slept since her talk with Emre. She'd practically staggered onto the docks and along the pier, but now her blood was flowing, returning to her some small amount of steadiness as she did her best to touch *not one bloody thing* on this strange ship.

"Adzin?" Emre called from behind her.

"Come, come," an effeminate voice answered from beyond the open doorway at the end of the hall.

They reached the doorway and found a room blessedly free of mad adornments. Within it stood a mouse of a man. He wore a black kaftan a bit too large for his frame. He had a pinched expression on his face, and his hands were clasped before him. Oddly, though, his left hand was massaging the meat of the opposite thumb, as if it had cramped. He regarded Emre with a flat expression. "You're Osman's man?"

Emre nodded, and Adzin turned to Çeda. "Which would make you the one."

Çeda hadn't been nervous about carrying so much money with her through the streets—she'd been too exhausted to worry over it—but she was nervous now. Adzin seemed the sort of man who would hardly think twice about driving the tip of a bent, broken awl into someone's kidney for a purse the size of the one she and Emre had brought for payment.

"I'm the one," she replied carefully.

"You have my coins?"

"We've come to find a man," Emre said.

Adzin moved behind a low table, where he reached up and pulled the string of a brass bell hanging from the thick wooden beam above him. The bell rang, the sound shrill in the cramped space of the cabin. Soon after, Çeda heard men dropping to the sand, felt the gentle tilt of the ship as it was towed away from the pier toward the harbor's center.

"I know very well what you've come to find, but I'll not discuss your quarry or anything else until the agreed-upon fee has been paid."

Emre swallowed hard. "I want a guarantee that the money's going to do her some good."

Adzin's eyes narrowed as he craned his neck forward. "How old are you?"

"Sixteen, my lord."

He looked Emre up and down. "Then perhaps you can be forgiven the insult. As Osman no doubt told you, I'm not in the business of *finding* anything until I know what you're about, and the one you wish to find besides. My time is valuable. Now set the coins on the table or jump this ship, because either way I'm headed for the desert."

Emre glanced sidelong at Çeda. After an unspoken agreement between the two of them, he took out two cloth purses from the larger leather one at his belt— months of meticulous savings from both Emre and Çeda—and dropped them onto a table that looked as if it had once served as a butcher's chopping block.

Adzin picked up the smaller one first, the one filled

with golden rahl. Apparently satisfied, he made it vanish into the folds of his kaftan. He then picked up the second, filled with lesser sylval, untying the drawstring with an intensity in his eyes that had been absent moments ago.

"All silver," Emre said, "as instructed."

As the ship turned, putting her on a heading that would take them toward the harbor's entrance, Adzin motioned to the dusty, threadbare pillows on the opposite side of the table. Emre and Çeda sat while Adzin lowered himself onto a large, overstuffed pillow with an Adzin-shaped indentation at its center. Then, with a deftness that made it clear he'd done this many times before, he upended the contents of the second purse and laid out the coins on the table one by one, making sure the faces of the various Kings of Sharakhai were exposed. After stuffing the empty purse into the sleeve of his kaftan, he turned each of the King's faces just so, though whether it was to do with the individual King or with the coin's position on the table, Çeda had no idea.

"Now"—he ran a pasty hand through his lank hair and regarded Çeda with a look he might use on a head of garlic he hadn't yet decided to buy—"this man you wish to find, tell me his name."

"Kadir," Çeda replied.

"His *full* name."

"I don't have it."

Adzin's beady eyes considered her, then he sniffed. "A proper name makes things easier but isn't necessary." He lifted his head to peer at her along his nose. "Why do you wish to find him, then, this Kadir?"

"The why of it isn't your concern," Emre replied. "I was told you could find those who needed finding. Now can you do it or can't you?"

"Well, I do need *something*," he said, as if the statement were self-evident. "Either give me his name, dear children, or tell me who he is."

Emre and Çeda exchanged a look. They'd come this far. What was a few more steps down this dark, winding path?

"He was the manservant of Rümayesh," Çeda said.

Adzin's dark expression clouded further. "Rümayesh."

Çeda nodded.

"She's—" Adzin visibly collected himself. "She's real, then?"

Çeda nodded again.

He licked his lips. "I was told nothing of this."

Emre looked ready to cut in with a sharp rebuke over Adzin's hesitance, so Çeda spoke quickly. "She will not be threatened in this. In fact, if all goes well, she may owe me, and those who helped, a great deal."

Adzin considered, then gave a short nod. "You said he *was* her manservant. What did you mean?"

"Rümayesh has gone missing," Çeda replied, "and Kadir went into hiding shortly after."

"And how would you weigh this man?"

"*Weigh* him?"

Adzin sniffed again, peering at her in that strange way of his. "Tell me the sort of man he was."

"Calm. Serious. Loyal."

"What were the qualities of his eyes?"

Çeda had to picture it in her mind, how he'd stood in that opulent meeting room where they'd first met. "Dark brown. Deep. He had a way of assessing you quickly."

"And the timbre of his voice?"

"Is this *necessary*?" Emre asked.

Çeda knew he was only trying to protect her, but she also knew how strange the ways of magic could be, so before Adzin could respond, she put her arm on Emre's and said, "His voice was rich. Powerful. The voice of a man accustomed to having his orders followed."

"And was it always so?"

Here, Çeda paused. What a strange question. How could she possibly know that? But when she thought about it, she wondered what sort of man he was before he'd met Rümayesh. He gave much to her, but had it always been so?

"I don't think so."

"Why?"

"I had the impression that Rümayesh chose him and brought him up, perhaps from the streets. There was a quality about him, as if he hadn't been born to the luxury of the estate where we spoke and was wondering even then when it all might vanish."

Adzin nodded. "Good," he said. "Good."

They continued for a time like this, the ship creaking as it heeled over the sand dunes, Adzin occasionally moving the sylval back into place when they slipped. Where they were headed Çeda had no idea. She only knew that Adzin was a man who, for an admittedly steep price, and for only the most carefully chosen clientele, would find things. She didn't even know *how* he did so, only that Emre had found him, Osman had vouched for him, and she'd become desperate enough to try anything at this point.

She might have tried looking for Kadir herself, but she was so exhausted she'd started seeing things from the corners of her eyes, hearing snippets of conversations when no one was in the room. She'd never find a man like Kadir in her current state. No, as much as Adzin made her skin crawl, and as dearly as this voyage was costing her, it was the only course of action that might net her quarry before Rümayesh's nightmares drove her mad.

Adzin's questions ranged from general to obscure. At

times he would pepper Çeda with them, and at others he would remain silent for minutes on end, staring at the coins arrayed before him. Through the small porthole to Çeda's left she could see night falling over the desert. An hour into their voyage, without warning, Adzin flipped each of the sylval over to show the sigil of the King whose face appeared on the opposite side, then continued his questioning as if nothing had happened. After several hours, the ship finally began to slow. Then it coasted to a stop. Soon after there came a rattle of chain and a thump as the ship's anchor stone dropped to the sand.

"Come," Adzin said.

With deft motions he swept up the coins and slipped them back into the same purse Emre had given him, then he stood and slipped past them, leading them out from the cabin, along the passageway that even in the darkness made Çeda's skin crawl, and up to the deck. The hulking deckhand dropped a rope ladder down to the sand, at which point Adzin, Çeda, and Emre climbed down and began walking toward a cluster of standing stones.

The sandy ground soon gave way to unforgiving rock. The evening wind was cool, but there was a strange scent upon it, like burnt wood and sulfur. As Adzin walked, he spoke. "There are still many of his creatures in the desert left behind from Goezhen's more active days crafting life of his own. They are much fewer after the great cleansing before the elder gods left for the farther fields, but they can be found if one knows where to look."

The twin moons were up, casting light bright enough to see two things: first, that there were giant stones set in a circle, and second, that within that circle lay a massive, gaping hole. Adzin led them past the stones, which were tall as trees, to the very edge of the hole. It dropped straight down, as if the elder gods had thrown a spear from the heavens to pierce the earth. The sulfurous smell became so unbearable Çeda was forced to cover her nose and mouth with her sleeve. Emre did the same. But Adzin merely kneeled at the edge of the hole and peered downward. What he might be looking for Çeda had no idea; it was so dark she couldn't see a thing.

Adzin was holding something now—their coin purse, the one filled with sylval—and he was whispering words to it.

Çeda tried to speak, but the smell made her choke.

"Be quiet," Adzin said, and continued to whisper. He dumped the coins carefully into his waiting palm. And then flung them with one swift motion, into the hole in the earth.

Emre gasped. Çeda's eyes widened and she ran to the edge of the hole despite the caustic smell. By the light of the moons she could see the coins spinning down, each glinting like the surface of a tiny moonlit pond. Away they fell, further and further, until finally they were lost from view.

Emre bristled. "By the gods, why would you—"

"Silence now!" Adzin barked.

He peered downward, leaning so far out over the edge Çeda thought he might tip over and spin, end over end like one of those coins, and be lost to the world forever more. He remained like this for a long while, long enough for Çeda to give up on seeing anything of note from where she stood, and she backed away, if only to grab a few breaths of comparatively pure air. Emre did the same. The two of them stared at one another, silently questioning what it was Adzin might be doing, and further, what they'd gotten themselves into.

That was when Çeda heard it. The flapping sound.

It was soft but soon grew until it sounded like the washer women in Sharakhai as they snapped their clothes before laying them to dry on sunbaked rocks. Something large flew up from the dark abyss. The creature's silhouette was difficult to discern against the gauze of stars, but it looked as though it had two sets of wings. Adzin raised one forearm like the falconer Çeda had once seen practicing for a show in the southern harbor. Moments later the creature flapped down and alighted on Adzin's outstretched arm, and he walked to where Çeda stood, whispering to the creature as he came. When he stood before her, he motioned for her to raise her arm. She did, while some unspeakable worry ate at her insides over this strange, foul-smelling creature.

"They're called ifin," Adzin said, pushing his arm against Çeda's until the ifin moved with ungainly steps onto Çeda's arm. "This one knows you now. More importantly, it knows this Kadir of yours. It knows his scent from the clues you've given me."

Çeda stared at the creature, her upper lip raising of its own accord. She felt like a wolf, hackles rising at something she couldn't understand. The ifin had a sinuous neck and a sleek, eyeless head, like a lamprey she'd seen once in the bazaar. Where its eyes should have been were strange patches of mosslike skin. The ifin's mouth looked like a funnel of bone-white teeth. Its four wings were like a bat's, leathery with grasping claws at the end of each. "What by the gods do I *do* with it?"

Adzin laughed. "Why, you bring it to Sharakhai. The ifin will do the rest."

———

With Emre by her side, Çeda staggered along a night-darkened street in Sharakhai, watching the ifin and the way ahead as carefully as her bleary eyes would allow. Adzin's ship had returned them to the city, and they were now making their way through its southeastern quarter, in a well-to-do neighborhood cut off from the city's most affluent areas by the dry bed of the Haddah. Where the ifin might be taking them she had no idea. She just hoped the bloody thing would stop faffing about and *do it*.

She stared into the darkness ahead, then looked about in a panic. Fucking gods, she'd lost the damned thing again.

"There," Emre said, pointing.

"Bless your sharp eyes," Çeda whispered.

The ifin was little more than a dark stain against the mudbrick of a three-story building farther up the lane. When Çeda and Emre neared, it launched itself into the sky, which was slowly brightening with the coming dawn. The strange beast circled three times, then flapped down the next street, its body wriggling like a sidewinding snake.

"You shit!" Çeda shouted. "You bloody fucking shit! We've been that way three times already!"

"Quiet!" Emre hissed. Then more calmly, "Adzin said it might do that."

"He also said the ifin would find Kadir by dawn if he could be found."

They'd been at this for hours, and Çeda was ready to collapse from fatigue. A dozen times already she'd walked into walls or scraped her arms or legs because she could no longer see straight. Everything kept going wavy on her, and sometimes she'd wake up paces from where she last remembered being, or on an entirely new street, not even realizing she'd fallen asleep.

"Nalamae's teats, Emre, I'm walking in my sleep."

"What?" Emre asked.

"Never mind." She stopped and put her hands on her knees, trying her best to wake up. "Maybe Adzin grabbed the wrong ifin."

"Only one answered the call. Come on." He took her arm, supporting her as he led her down the street where the ifin had flown. "One way or the other, it'll be over soon."

They followed the ifin and found it atop a bronze statue of one of Sharakhai's Kings—she couldn't remember which. The statue stood in a dry fountain, shamshir raised high, the ifin circling the King's turban as if it were about to nest. *Or take a shit,* Çeda thought. Its twin pair of wings flapped slowly, its head swinging this way and that, smelling or tasting, or in some other way sensing its quarry.

"What if he's gone, Emre?" The very thought made her want to fall to her knees and weep. "What if he's dead?"

"The ifin wouldn't follow a trail that led to a dead man."

"After those ridiculous questions Adzin was asking? I don't know." Any confidence she might have had while speaking with Adzin on the ship had long since vanished, replaced with a growing certainty that they'd been sent on a fool's errand, or worse, swindled out of a year's worth of pay.

She looked back up to the winged demon, wondering if it was actually sensing anything. Fucking thing was probably laughing at how much money it had helped its master to steal from them.

"It might not matter what the damned ifin does," she said weakly.

"Why?"

Çeda swung her head toward Emre. "What?"

"You just said it might not matter."

"Oh." She pinched her eyes tight and licked her lips. "It's just . . . I'm going to collapse, Emre. I can hardly keep one foot plodding in front of the other. I can't take another night of those dreams."

But Emre was no longer looking at her. He was staring at the statue. The flutter of the ifin's wings filled the cold morning air as it took flight. "Why don't you let me chase it? Go home, and I'll return when it's done."

She shook her head. "Can't, Emre. What if it's using me to find Kadir?"

In the predawn light, she couldn't see Emre's face well, but she could tell he was frowning. "I hadn't thought of that."

She pulled herself up and took as deep a breath as she could manage. "Let's go. I'll last for a while yet."

They chased the ifin down another street, waited while it rested on a lamppost outside a tavern, then down a gap between two buildings so narrow the two of them had to sidestep through it, and along a paved walkway that hugged the dry southern bank of the Haddah.

When the ifin flew across the riverbed, however, a chill ran down her frame. The creature had been mercurial before, like a butterfly flitting here then there, but now it was flying straight, with purpose, it seemed to Çeda, and it was heading in a direction that Çeda thought would be one of the last places Kadir might be found. Why, though? Why would he have returned to that place?

Settle yourself, Çeda. You don't yet know if that's where he's gone.

They continued to a wide, well-kept road, the terminus of a winding street that ran between several of the city's smaller estates. If the Kings of Sharakhai could be said to draw wealth and power like roots drew water at the base of some grand tree, these families were the stout branches that benefited from it. Kadir had rubbed elbows with these people for his mistress, so the fact that the ifin was headed to the richest quarter of Sharakhai aside from the House of Kings itself wasn't surprising. What *was* surprising, though, was the fact that it appeared to be headed for the very same estate where Rümayesh had performed her strange ritual on Çeda. Indeed, in little time, the ifin flew over the wall Çeda had scaled to escape.

"This is it," Çeda whispered, stopping at the iron gates and pointing to the estate house. The ifin sat upon a low hill like a sleeping jackal.

"Where she took you?"

"Yes." Çeda peered over the grounds. The small guardhouse on the inside of the gate appeared to be unmanned. She searched for the ifin, but couldn't see it in the darkness.

"Kadir came back then," Emre said.

"Yes," Çeda said. "The only question is why." She spotted the ifin circling in the sky. Far to the right, beyond a low stone wall, lay the mausoleums, the boneyard of the rich. "Come."

She climbed the gate and dropped inside, only then seeing the form lying near the gatehouse. She approached and found a guard wearing light mail lying there, alive but unconscious. She and Emre shared a look. The sun would rise soon, and the gods only knew when the guard might awaken. They made their way quickly toward the peaked roofs, and soon they were weaving between the mausoleums, looking up to the ifin to find the one it had sensed for them.

Soon it became obvious. Ahead, the door to the mausoleum from which Çeda had escaped was cracked open. The moment she touched the door, the ifin released a short, piercing, skin-tingling cry and flew westward. It was soon lost beyond the stone roofs of the mausoleums. Çeda glanced at Emre, then stepped inside. Ahead was a hallway leading to the dark, open maws of a dozen crypts, while to her left was the set of stairs that led down to the room where Rümayesh's ritual had been performed. Soft, golden light rose from it like the coming of dawn.

Her heart beat heavy in her chest. For once, the exhaustion that had lain across her shoulders like a leaden mantle was gone—supplanted by fear.

They took the stairs down. Çeda drew her kenshar, gripped it tightly in one hand. Emre did the same, his eyes bright moons in the ghastly light. They reached the level below, where a room opened up before them, most of it lost in darkness. At the far side was a lone doorway, and through it Çeda could see a man leaning over an open sarcophagus, the very one that had hidden Rümayesh from the world as she wore the skin of the beautiful matron of this estate. Of the moths, thankfully, there was no sign. The very thought of them brought the memories of that harrowing night to Çeda's mind. She pushed them away and focused on the room ahead.

The man, of course, was Kadir. By the light of the lantern that lay on the sarcophagus lid, his lissome form was reaching inside, one arm making sawing motions.

Rümayesh couldn't still be here. The boys had her. Somewhere. Certainly not here. So what in the great, wide desert was Kadir doing?

Çeda strode forward. The floors and walls of the crypt were blackened—by blood, by fire, by the burnt remains of the irindai moths. Kadir jumped when she entered the light, then turned to meet her approach with a long, gleaming kenshar in his left hand. As he took her in, his eyes softened. He lowered his knife, but sent wary glances toward Emre when he stood beside her.

Çeda stepped closer to the sarcophagus. Inside was a woman's form, swathed in white gauze. Vials of amber and myrrh and vetiver were gripped in the woman's hands. Dried river flowers were sprinkled over her form. The cloth around her left foot, however, had been cut by Kadir, exposing her foot and ankle.

"What are you doing?" Çeda said, her words sharp and brittle in this hard, confined space.

Kadir stared as if trying to weigh her, to know her mind as Rümayesh might have done, though whether he *had* some similar ability, and if so, had succeeded or not, Çeda couldn't tell. She crossed her arms over her chest. "Rümayesh sent me."

Kadir shivered. "She what?"

"She sent me here." She told him of the dreams she'd been having. She told him of the cold room, the strange ridge with the dead trees. She told him how Rümayesh had called out his name when Hidi had begun torturing her. "She *wanted* me to find you. The only question is why."

Kadir looked around the room, calculating. When he met Çeda's eyes again, he seemed to have come to some decision. "She needs you to find her."

Çeda shook her head. "She needs *you*. That's why she sent me to find you."

Kadir waggled his head, granting her the point, but only grudgingly. "She needs us both." Before Çeda could protest, he raised one hand, then pointed to the interior of the sarcophagus with the tip of the knife. "Come look."

He took the lamp and lifted the woman's foot so that the light shone brightly against the exposed skin. A tattoo was imprinted upon the sole: *In the room of golden reflections, beneath a heart of stone.*

"It's the location of her sigil stone," Kadir said.

Her sigil stone. The place where her name, her true name, was imprinted. "It's what the boys are after," Çeda whispered.

Kadir nodded.

"But how . . . Why is it here," Çeda motioned to the tattoo, "on the sole of some woman's foot?"

Kadir held the lantern still, staring into Çeda's eyes, waiting for her to stitch the clues together.

"It's a message," Emre said, stepping more fully into the light.

"She walked this form," Çeda said, the pieces falling into place. "It's a message to you, if her form dies."

Kadir nodded. "You'll recall Rümayesh left this place under . . . unusual circumstances. Because of your actions, the woman did not in fact die when Rümayesh left her form."

"She's dead now," Çeda said plainly.

Kadir slipped the knife into the sheath at his belt and seemed to choose his next words with care. "Her soul took a bit of convincing before it agreed to depart these shores."

Gods, Kadir killed her, or at the very least *arranged* for her to be killed, all so that he could come here and find this secret: the location of Rümayesh's sigil stone. Could he not have simply drugged her? She looked to Kadir and considered the question, and came to the conclusion that he had been chosen as much for his ruthlessness as for his attentive care of his mistress. With Rümayesh taken, he likely wanted no additional complications.

Kadir set the lantern down and began heaving the sarcophagus's lid back into place. It set home with a boom. "Do you know how to ride a horse?"

"Poorly," Çeda replied. "Why? Where are we going?"

"We can talk freely in the desert. I have a horse that is well trained. He'll offer you no trouble."

It was clear he meant for Çeda to join him alone.

"I'm coming as well," Emre said as Kadir took up the lantern and headed for the stairs. "I'm coming as well!" He repeated to Kadir's retreating form. He made to follow, but Çeda blocked his path.

"Let me ride with him, Emre."

"I'll not leave you."

Çeda knew the information she wanted from Kadir would be difficult for him to share, which meant she needed him as pliant as possible, so, while she hated to do it, she took Emre's hand and held it tenderly. "We're going to talk and he's going to help. That's all."

"Then let him do it while I ride with you. I can ride farther back if he's worried about me hearing."

"He doesn't trust you, but he knows I'm wrapped up in this as deeply as he is." She leaned in and kissed his cheek. "You've done me a great service in bringing me this far. Now return home so I can finish what we've started. I'll return as soon as I'm able."

Emre wasn't happy about it, but he finally agreed. He

squeezed her hand, and together they headed toward the stairwell, which dimmed like the sunset as Kadir treaded higher.

———

Leagues east of Sharakhai, Kadir rode on a horse with a golden coat, an akhala, a rare breed widely considered the finest in the desert. Çeda bounced along behind him on a silver mare with a mane of copper, one of the most beautiful horses she'd ever seen, which made it all the more galling that it refused to bow to her will. A horse this beautiful ought to have better manners, and despite Kadir's assurances that the horse was sweet-tempered, the beast was constantly pulling at the bridle, turning left when it pleased when it was clear to god and man alike that Çeda was asking it to follow alongside Kadir's horse.

As they rode deeper into the desert, Kadir told her of his flight from the estate after Rümayesh had been taken by Hidi and Makuo. He'd stolen into the tomb several days later, finding it both empty and clean—as if by doing so the matron could wipe away her memories of the bloodshed. He'd searched for Rümayesh across the city, hoping to find her in one of the places they'd called home these past many years.

"Were you young when you joined her?" Çeda asked.

Kadir reined his horse up and motioned for Çeda to

do the same. He urged his horse into a walk, guiding it along the trail behind them. Reaching into one of the saddle bags, he scooped a handful of salt and sprinkled it over the tracks of their horses, a thing he'd done twice already on their ride out from Sharakhai. When he returned to her side, his golden akhala shaking its reins momentarily, he said, "Yes, I was young. What of it?"

"It's only . . . I'm surprised she would place her life in your hands. In *anyone's* hands."

Kadir merely shrugged. "We share a mutual trust in one another."

Ahead, Çeda could see a swath of land that looked strangely shadowed, as if dark clouds hung over it. The sky, though, was blue as blue could be. As they rode closer, Çeda understood. The shadows were actually the trunks of long-dead trees, hundreds, thousands of them.

As they neared the border of the strange forest, the ground became dusty and dry. The air smelled acrid, like a smithy's forge. No boughs graced the petrified remains of the trees. No branches. Only the trunks remained, standing like the spears of long-dead soldiers, the men who once wielded them gripping the hafts from within their earthen graves. More than this, though, the place felt cursed, as if it once had been a place gifted with rain and rich soil, a respite from the harshness of the Great

Shangazi, but one day the desert had tired of it and come to reclaim it.

The two of them rode into the dead forest. Çeda's skin went immediately cold. "Where are we going?" she asked.

He scooped another handful of salt, rode behind, and sprinkled it along their path. "Not much farther now."

He hadn't answered the question, but she was too tired to argue. She already knew this was the place from her dreams, the place Rümayesh was being kept, and for now that was enough.

Kadir led them a quarter-league farther, then reined his horse short. He slipped from the saddle with practiced ease and tied the reins around one of the thinner trunks. Çeda lumbered down from her saddle and did the same, after which Kadir led them east. As they walked, the only sound was that of the rocky soil crunching beneath their boots; nothing else, not even the sigh of the wind, broke the oppressive stillness, and it was making her feel as though everything in the desert for leagues around could hear them.

"Come," Çeda said, if only to break the unnatural silence. "I don't enjoy games. Tell me why we've come."

"You know already that the godlings are looking for Rümayesh's sigil stone, the piece of obsidian upon which Rümayesh's name was written."

"Because they wish to control her."

Kadir nodded, granting her the point. "I was worried they'd been sent to kill her, but after you told me she was alive, and that they were torturing her, I think it likely they plan to take her to their father, Onondu. With her true name they could make her a slave to the God of the Endless Hills, a thing he would no doubt enjoy immensely."

Rümayesh, in a way, had tried to enslave Çeda. She'd been trying to take Çeda's memories from her and hand them out like bites of some rich dessert. It was an unforgivable thing, and yet Çeda had to admit there was a part of her that cringed at the thought of allowing Hidi and Makuo to do the same to Rümayesh. There might be slave blocks in Sharakhai—a concession to the trade that occurred there between the border kingdoms—but the desert itself had none; it was a thing too barbaric even for the cruel Kings of Sharakhai to allow. And, she had to admit, she owed the twins a strange sort of debt. She might have been a plaything in their schemes, but they'd also shown her the path to escaping that crypt with her mind and soul intact.

Through the dead columns of trees, Çeda could see they were coming to some sort of drop-off or cliff. Before they reached it, Kadir dropped salt on their trail one more time and motioned Çeda to lay flat on the ground. She did, and together the two of them slithered over the rocky ground to the edge. A valley opened up below them. It was neither wide nor deep, and was largely filled with scrub trees and wiry stands of grass and stone the same red color as the ground upon which they lay. But in the valley's center was a keep with a tall tower.

"She is there," Çeda said.

Kadir nodded. "Your dreams confirmed it for me. But that isn't all. The stone lies within that place."

"The stone is *there*?"

"Along the south side of the keep lies a room with golden mirrors. It's what the tattoo meant. In the room of golden reflections, beneath a heart of stone. The stone is hidden there."

"Then the boys must know."

"Not necessarily."

"Why else would they have come here, to this place of all places?"

"Rümayesh may have convinced them to come. She has a way of making others do things without them even realizing it."

"That's madness. Why would she bring them any-where near her sigil stone when it's the very thing they want?"

Without taking his eyes from the keep, Kadir smiled wickedly. "Because she knows I'm searching for her, and that if I'm able, I will see her reborn."

"Don't take me for a fool, Kadir. The ehrekh are not reborn. Their names were given to them at the moment of their birth by Goezhen himself. If one finds such a name, the ehrekh will come to heel. I've read the stories. I've asked those who know."

Some moments passed before Kadir responded. "Did you know that man is imbued with a trace of blood from the elder gods?"

Çeda shrugged, curious why he would mention it. "Everyone knows that."

"Many know, yes. What most are blissfully unaware of is that it is the very presence of elder blood that makes the ehrekh hunger for us. Why many of them toy with us as they do." He paused, eyeing the tower as the wind played at its foot, making the sand there twist and spin like a demon. "Most ehrekhs' names were engraved upon stones on the day Goezhen first gave them breath, and I suspect the same was true for Rümayesh the day *she* was made. Most have one name and one name only. It is all they will ever have. But Rümayesh found a way around this. And all it takes is someone, anyone, with the will to give of their blood."

"Who would do that? It would make them beholden to her."

"You're right in a way you will probably never comprehend, but it isn't merely Rümayesh who gains in this arrangement. The man or woman gains as well. They are given much through this pact." As he spoke these words there was a hunger in his eyes, as if he'd long thought on this.

"Your blood marks her stone, doesn't it?" Çeda said.

"Mine?" Kadir laughed. "No. That is a power I do not wish for myself."

"But you'll do it now? To free her?"

"No, I will not." He stared at her intently, with meaning.

And Çeda suddenly understood. "You want *me* to do it?"

Kadir nodded.

"I won't."

"There's little choice left. You and Rümayesh are already bonded, a thing you're well aware of. You are linked inextricably, your fates entwined until you untwine them. If she is taken to Kundhun, you must follow. You'll be enslaved as she will be. Or if you somehow manage to resist the call and remain in Sharakhai, you'll be driven mad with yearning."

Çeda closed her eyes. *Gods, what have I gotten myself into?* She wanted to be anywhere but here. She resented what Rümayesh had done, resented the fact that she was now beholden to an ehrekh. But she was where she was. There was no sense hiding from it.

"What must I do?" she asked Kadir.

"You'll need to find the stone within the room of mirrors. Find it, then use your blood to wipe away the mark you'll find on the stone's surface. I'll find you a stone upon which you'll write a new name, also in blood, the old blood mixing with the new. When you speak that name, Rümayesh will be reborn. She will be freed from the bonds the godling twins have placed on her."

"And then?"

"And then, Rümayesh will return the favor to those boys."

"I mean for me. What happens to *me* then?"

"You may find her distasteful, but you will not find her ungrateful. She will let you leave, of this I'm sure, likely with a boon of your own choosing."

"I wish for no boon. I want only to be left alone."

Kadir touched his hands to his forehead, as the servants of the wealthy did. "Without doubt, it will be as you say."

Words, Çeda thought as they crept away from the cliff's edge. *Empty words.* As useful to her as a third eye. "I'll need money."

They rose and began walking back toward the horses. "I didn't take you for a mercenary."

"It isn't for me. It's to buy the help I'll need, and it won't come cheap."

Kadir paused, but then shrugged. "Whatever you need, I'll supply."

———

Çeda entered a shisha den along the Trough and found Brama sitting on the far side of the long front room. He was lounging on pillows, leaning over the table speaking with some Malasani harlot with a chain running between one of a dozen earrings and her nose ring. She was Brama's age, sixteen, maybe seventeen years old. As Çeda wove between the piles of pillows and the few patrons drawing breath from snaking shisha tubes, the girl reached out and brushed one of Brama's curly brown locks behind his ear.

They were not friends, Çeda and Brama, but through her haze of exhaustion she still felt poorly about what had happened between them after he'd stolen Osman's purse from her. She also felt a pang of guilt for coming to him unannounced. This couldn't wait, though. It had to be done tonight.

"Brama," she called as she drew near.

Brama turned to her, clearly annoyed, but when he saw who it was, his expression hardened. "What do *you* want?"

"I need a favor, Brama."

"A *favor?*"

Çeda's eyes flicked toward the girl. "A favor."

"I'm not inclined to grant favors, Çeda, least of all to you."

"Consider it business, then." She took the cinched leather purse from the pouch at her belt and tossed it through the air. She hoped it would be enough. She'd filled it with the last of her coin, plus a bit from Kadir, who hadn't had much on him when she left him.

Brama caught the purse with a snap of his hand. "What's this?"

She bowed from the waist. "Enough money to gain me an audience with his Highness, I'll wager."

Brama weighed the purse in his hand, glanced to the Malasani girl, then to Çeda. "Order some tea, my lovely. I'll be back presently." The girl smiled like some moon-eyed calf—it was so forced it made Çeda want to gag—but as soon as Brama's back was turned she stared daggers at Çeda. When they'd reached the alley behind the den, Brama spun to face her. "Now what do you want?"

"I need a lockslip. I figure after what happened between us you wouldn't want to do it yourself, but you know others." It wasn't exactly what she was after, but she couldn't very well go straight at him. "It'll pay well, Brama."

"Go to Osman if you need someone."

"Osman doesn't need to know anything about this." She pointed at the purse he still held in his hand. "There's more for the one who takes up the job. And gold to follow, assuming things end well."

As Brama stared, his expression softened from naked distrust to calculated nonchalance. She hid the relief spreading through her. He was interested, and that was by far the toughest step.

He seemed to take more note of her—her eyes, her hair. "You don't look well." He hoisted the purse up. "Is it to do with this?"

"I haven't been sleeping."

Brama laughed wickedly. "Tell me another secret, Çeda. You look like a scrap of leather that's been worried by the foulest hounds in all the desert."

"This is dark business," Çeda said, ignoring the insult. "Might get dangerous."

He shrugged, a gesture that said *I can take anything that you can* as clearly as if he'd spoken the words. "Might cost you a bit more, then, but I'm not afraid of a bit of danger."

"That's why I came to you first." She paused as the wind in the alley swirled, kicking up sand and dust, making her turn her head until it passed. The air smelled of roasting meat. When she spoke again, she did so very softly. "Do you know what an ehrekh is, Brama?"

"Enough to say the price just went up."

Çeda went on to explain what she needed to do. Not all of it, but enough for Brama to get the gist: a trip to the desert, steal into a keep, find the sigil stone, all as quickly as they could manage. They would do it late in the afternoon, the most likely time for the godling boys to be resting. She tried to avoid talking about the stone, what she meant to do with it, but Brama pressed, and she didn't wish for him to become suspicious, so she told him about the blood ritual Kadir had described, erasing the old sigil with blood, the crafting of a new one on a second obsidian stone.

When Çeda had finished, Brama considered her for a time. "All of this to free an ehrekh?"

"To free *myself*."

Brama shifted his weight on his hips, scratched at the brown fuzz along his jaw that might one day become a beard. "They grant wishes, you know."

"The ehrekh? No, they don't, Brama. They're wicked, and they'll kill you if you cross them."

"The stories all tell of wishes, Çeda."

As if Brama knew the first thing about them. "Those are tales that grew in the telling. We're to get in, remake her stone, and leave. That's all."

"You're going to use *your* blood on the stone, then? Put *yourself* in danger?"

"I'm already *in* danger, so why not?"

"What's the payoff, then?"

"Two hundred rahl."

Brama laughed. "You don't have two gold coins to rub together, Çeda."

"Kadir is the one who'll be paying you, not me."

"And why would *he* pay for *you*?"

"He's paying for his mistress, Rümayesh. He would see her freed from these boys."

Brama considered. "Two hundred?"

"In gold as bright as the sun, Brama."

After a pause in which Brama looked her up and down, as if that might give him some sort of insight, he nodded. "How do we know when it'll be safe to enter?"

"I dream," Çeda said, her stomach already beginning to turn, "and then we wait for Makuo to come with his knife."

———

Cold desert air falling across her skin.

The scent of wood coals burning.

A soft rattle, a sound she knows all too well—the blade of a knife being thrust beneath hot coals, the beginning of its short journey to a flaming brand. It brings with it a host of memories, a menagerie of endless, pain-filled nights spent with these trickster boys, the sons of Onondu.

They've placed bonds upon her, preventing her from slipping away from her keep, the place where she'd first taken breath. But even Onondu's power cannot prevent her from retreating deep into her mind. Each time the boys have come with their wicked smiles and their glowing blades, she has hidden herself, but her place of refuge has been more difficult to reach of late, as if the episodes of pain are in fact bricks being stacked at its entrance. Soon, she knows, the bricks will stand too high, and she will be blocked from reaching its sheltering darkness altogether.

And then—no matter what she might wish—she will deliver to these boys the thing they've been searching for all along.

She lifts her head and peers about the room.

Only one of the boys is here, standing in the corner, his back to her, staring down at the brazier where the knife rests in the dull red coals. It is Hidi, she is sure. The one who enjoys this work too dearly to give the knife to his brother.

When Hidi turns to her, knife in hand, his face is lit by the glow of the blade. "I feel the cracks in you." She can see his eyes, his lips, the river trail of the scar running from his temple and down one cheek. "The knife and the heat tearing down the walls. I know it. You know it, too, yes?"

He reaches her side. The chains clink as she tries to scramble back, but she is bound, not only by the black iron, but by the wards these boys have placed around her on the floor.

Hidi circles the tip of the blade over her cheek, as if choosing where he might press first. "Will they fall tonight?" He leans in, smiling a smile that is anything but innocent. "Why fight, though? We find your secret sooner or later. So you give it, yes? And we go. We go to my father and you see. He be nice to you. In time you like the grasslands, forget about the endless sands in this hot, hot place."

She has felt pain in her long life—Goezhen forged her to endure much—but the pain this boy is ready to deal, on top of what she's already been through, is nearly too much.

Months ago she would laugh at the very notion of fearing these boys, but here, lying helpless before one who tears at her flesh and teases her with empty promises that seem real enough to grasp . . . It's enough to make the foundation of her resolve crumble.

She tries to find that hidden place again, but the growing terror prevents her from leaving.

"It's . . ."

"What?" Hidi asks, his eyes bright.

Goezhen save me, I nearly told him.

"Come, come. Tell Hidi, and it will *all* end. Tell me where your sigil hides."

She could end it. Hidi might even be telling her the truth. She might go to Kundhun and live with Onondu's yoke around her neck. She could bide her time and find a way to leave. She might even kill the God of the Endless Hills to teach all in the desert that no one trifles with Goezhen's children, not even a god.

She swallows hard, knowing these thoughts for what they are: false hopes, one and all. Give herself to Onondu and she would die in that foreign place.

She swallows, tries to flee one last time, but it's no use. That path has been closed.

"It's gone," she says at last. "Stolen from me centuries ago by a thief." The lie she's told him from the beginning. She can manage this much, at least, even if it only delays the inevitable.

Her answer displeases Hidi.

His eyes harden as the blade lowers.

And then the pain begins.

"Çeda!"

Çeda opened her eyes to darkness.

She lay in bed, in her home in Sharakhai. A man

loomed over her, one hand clamped tightly over her mouth, the other shaking her violently.

Emre?

"Çeda, for the love of the gods, wake up!"

No. Not Emre at all.

Someone else. A boy with a wicked grin.

She looked about for the glowing knife. She fought. She struck the boy across the jaw, and when he recoiled from the blow she kicked him as hard as she could.

As he grunted and fell backward, it all came back in a rush. The trip to the desert. Falling asleep as the stars came out. Dreaming the dream of an ehrekh.

She wasn't home in her bed; she was sleeping among the trees of the strange forest where Kadir had once taken her. And the man she'd just kicked was no godling boy, but Brama.

Brama reached his feet, then rubbed his jaw. His stance was wary, but when she made no move to attack, he stood tall and glared down at her while the silver light of Rhia shone down half-lidded from the heavens.

As memories of the pain Hidi had been inflicting faded at last, the wounds on her own face registered. Her lip was split, and the right side of her face felt as if she'd just finished a particularly nasty bout in the pits. "Well you didn't have to beat me like a stubborn mule!"

"You were *screaming*! Do you think they'll not hear us? You might wish to suffer the same fate as your ehrekh, but *I* certainly don't. Now get up. It's time to go."

Brama rolled up his blanket, cinching it tightly.

Çeda began to do the same, but stopped when Brama went to tie the blanket behind the saddle of his horse. Çeda quickly opened the locket around her neck and took out one of the adichara petals hidden within. She placed it beneath her tongue, closed the locket, then helped tear down their makeshift camp. The petal's flavor was strange, like sour ale, so unlike its normally bright taste, and it did little more than allow her aching body to move with something approaching normalcy. It would have to be enough, she decided. She'd been taking the petals so often she wasn't surprised the effects weren't as strong as usual.

She finished preparing the horses and then strapped her shamshir across her back, and pulled the veil of her turban into place. "Ready," she said to Brama.

Brama had two lengths of rope wound crosswise around one shoulder and across his chest. Other implements like metal hooks and several small bags hung from his belt, the tools of his trade. "You don't *sound* ready, and by the gods you don't look ready, either."

She shrugged. "I'm as ready as I'll ever be."

"You have the stone?"

Çeda placed her hand on the leather pouch at her belt. Within rested the obsidian disk Kadir had given to her. "I have it." Kadir himself had refused to join them, saying there were other things that needed doing should they succeed in the keep. What those things might be, he had refused to say.

"Very well," Brama said, and with that he set off at a brisk jog. "Keep up, Çeda. The run will do you good."

She followed, and together they threaded their way through the stone tree trunks toward the drop-off where Kadir led her yesterday. They'd debated on whether to bring the horses nearer. Having them close might be handy in a pinch, but Brama had reasoned that if the twins were as dangerous as she said, then leaving them back a bit was the wiser course. She'd agreed, but now she regretted the decision. She was so exhausted she kept brushing up against the trees, and once a branch caught her hip and twisted her around as she ran. As she fell hard to the dry, packed earth, she could swear it sounded as though someone were laughing in the distance, but when she stood and glanced back along her path, she saw nothing. The trunks of all the trees were bare.

Brama came running back and immediately held his hand out, motioning for the pouch at her belt. "Çeda, I should do this alone. Give the stone to me and I'll return as soon as it's done."

"No," Çeda said, her hand on the pouch. "That isn't why I brought you."

"You're ready to collapse!"

"I only tripped is all."

Brama stood there for the span of a breath, then said, "If you say so," and spun on his boot heels and continued toward the cliff. Çeda followed, moving slower now, wary of the trees, wary of Brama as well.

When they arrived at the cliff, Brama tied one length of rope around the nearest of the dead trees, threw the bulk of it down the slope, and climbed after it. Çeda followed, and the two of them soon reached a stone lip, which was the point at which the decline became more manageable. Silver Tulathan was high in the night sky now. Golden Rhia was rising. By their light Çeda and Brama picked their way carefully down to avoid a fall, and soon reached the valley floor, where they ran quick and low toward the keep.

Çeda could hear the screams from the tower now. She could see the ruddy light from the brazier as well. She rubbed her thigh where Hidi had plunged the knife into Rümayesh's thigh. It hurt *Çeda's* leg now, made her move with ungainly steps. Çeda grunted as pain burned deep into the muscle of her other leg, too—a fresh wound from Hidi, surely, some echo of what Rümayesh was feeling in that room high in the tower.

Brama turned. She could see the worry in his face. He pulled her upright, looking toward the slope they'd just descended. "You're going to get us both killed, Çeda."

"I'll be *fine*," she said through gritted teeth.

He looked as though he were ready to send her back anyway, but then he turned and continued toward the keep. Çeda followed, muffling her pain as well as she was able, the feelings in her body an echo of the screams coming from the tower above. When they reached the wall, Brama ran his hands over the stones with unexpected tenderness. Like a master huntsman might choose a path through a forest, his gaze moved along the stones, ever upward, toward the battlements. He did this a second time, then a third, and finally set his fingers into the gaps between the stones and began to scale the wall.

The keep was old, the stones of the wall weathered, and yet when Brama began climbing, he did so as if the task were no harder than crawling along the ground. His grip was sure and strong, his instincts perfect. He placed his feet just so, used his arms to draw himself ever higher, and he paused only long enough for his fingers to find purchase in the gaps, however slight they might be. As quickly as he was moving, each moment seemed an age, for Rümayesh's outpouring of pain filled Çeda with every breath, every beat of her heart.

Hurry, Brama. Please.

When he reached the top, he wrapped the remaining rope around a merlon and sent it snaking down to Çeda. She tried to climb, but was forced to allow Brama to pull her up as a new sort of pain—the kind that made you forget *who* you were and *where* you were—was driven deep into her gut. She groaned as the cries of anguish coming from the tower rose to new heights. The misery of an ehrekh poured from it, along with the glee of a godling child, and Çeda *felt* that pain, a mere echo of what Rümayesh was feeling now. How by the gods' sweet breath could anyone, even an ehrekh, endure the torture being delivered?

The moment Brama dragged her over the battlements, Çeda collapsed to the rampart.

"Stay here," Brama said. "I'll return with the stone."

Çeda grabbed the leg of his trousers. The pain was decreasing at last. She could hear words drifting down from the window in the tower above, could hear some soft echo of them inside her mind as well. Hidi. Though what he was saying Çeda couldn't tell.

"I can make it," she said.

"Then *get up*. I'm not staying in this infernal place for a moment longer than I need to."

After coiling the rope, Brama dropped it along the inside of the wall and slipped down to the keep's barren courtyard. Çeda followed, and soon the two of them were gliding like ghosts to the door at the far side, the one Kadir had told her to find. Brama knelt, lock picks at the ready. He slipped them into the keyhole and moved them carefully while pressing his ear to the door. Soon the door was open and Brama was helping her to stand.

The hall that greeted them was dark, but Kadir had described the keep well enough. After a series of passages, they came to a lone, unlocked door at the end of a hall. The room inside was lit faintly by open windows high above. The walls—as the message tattooed on the sole of the woman's foot had implied—were covered with golden mirrors.

No sooner did Çeda step inside than—thank Nalamae for her grace—the pain in her body lifted. She was able to breathe deeply, and instead of curling inward from the agony in her gut and chest, was able to stand tall for the first time in what felt like years.

Çeda stared at the mirrors, wondering at the properties of this room. A sanctum of sorts? A place for Rümayesh to escape from the world?

Brama had already moved to the center of the room, which was littered with dust, stacked furniture, and mismatched piles of books that looked as if they'd been ransacked, though whether that was recently or ages ago, Çeda couldn't tell. Brama knelt and swept his hands over the stones, examining each in turn. Çeda joined him, looking for the stone the tattoo had described—*beneath a heart of stone*, it had said. It took little time for her to find it, a stone the size and shape of a human heart.

"Here," she said. It pried up easily, revealing a deep hole. She reached in and found a bag made from cloth-of-gold, and when she tugged at the neck and upended it, an obsidian disk fell onto her palm. It was dark and clear. It reflected moonlight like glass. Upon its surface was an ancient symbol, a complex sigil that represented Rümayesh. It was her name, but also, to a degree, her entire *identity*. Kadir had told her she must wipe it away and create another, and through that ritual she would somehow *define* the ehrekh and trigger a rebirth.

Brama watched her with a hungry expression. *"Hurry!"* he hissed when he finally had her attention.

The edges of the obsidian were rough, almost knife-like. She used it to make a cut along the palm of her left hand, then collected the blood on her opposite thumb and rubbed it along the surface of the disk, mixing it with the dried blood there.

As she did, a wind began to whisper through the windows above. The wind's intensity quickly grew. It began to howl, to whine. Dust and sand swirled at the center of the room. Silver moonlight cut through the dust and sand like spears cast down by Tulathan herself.

"What are you waiting for? Get the other stone." Brama's voice was high-pitched, his face a study in worry.

Çeda dug in her purse for the stone, but stopped when she heard the scuff of steps behind her. She spun and found a dark-skinned boy standing in the doorway.

"You not find it there," Makuo said.

He was holding an obsidian disk, she realized. She reached deeper inside her purse and pulled out a hunk of sandstone. She stared at it, confused, but then realized what it was that had caught her and made her fall out in the dead forest. Makuo. He'd been there, and he'd switched the stone without her realizing it.

"You come," Makuo said, laughing, "like we know *nothing*, like we birds sitting in a tree, waiting to be taken by a stone from your sling." He sent the disk spinning into the air with a flick of his wrist. "What you think now, girl? Are we birds waiting to be struck?"

Too late, she remembered what she'd forgotten from her dream. Makuo hadn't been in the tower room. Hidi had come alone. Gods, how foolish of her . . . But her mind had been so addled from lack of sleep, and from the jarring shift of perception when Brama had pummeled her awake.

Had the twins known all along about her dreams? Had they allowed her to continue so that she and Brama would reveal the location of the sigil stone? Had *Kadir* known and put her at risk for some other purpose?

What matter is any of that now?

Makuo opened the door and shouted down the hall. "Come, brother! The girl here, and she bring a friend."

As he did this, Çeda saw something from the corner of her eye. The moons were high, their light shining through the windows above. In one of the mirrors, she saw a man. Kadir. In the reflection, he was standing just next to her, but he wasn't here in this moonlit room. She could see other things that didn't match as well—furniture, paintings on the walls, a woven rug, none of which appeared in *this* room, all cast golden by the mirror's surface.

A portal, Çeda realized.

The mirror was a portal, and Kadir was on the opposite side, waiting for the right time to step through it.

She reached for her shamshir as Makuo was turning around.

"Looking for this?" The boy laughed bitterly as he tossed Çeda's curving shamshir into the hall behind him, where it clattered against the stones. "This, too?" He flipped his empty hand into the air, and suddenly, Çeda's kenshar was spinning in the air. He caught it with a flick of his wrist. "You think you take *my* blood? No, girl, Makuo take *yours*. Makuo mark the sigil stone with it and bind you to Rümayesh before you die."

Çeda didn't wait for any more words.

She charged.

She knew Makuo was quick, that he was gifted with the trick of disappearing and reappearing, and so she was ready when a shadow was cast over the doorway and he vanished. She spun and found him thrusting the dagger toward her.

She sidestepped. Swept both hands in a blocking motion across his wrist and used his momentum to whip him down to the floor. He struck the stones hard and grunted as his breath was expelled. He tried to twist his arm free, but Çeda held tight. She used her advantage to climb atop his back while keeping the knife at bay.

Brama came running, knifepoint down as he prepared to stab Makuo. But Makuo had godsblood running through his veins. He was strong and wickedly quick. He kicked Brama's legs out from underneath him, then twisted in a furious motion, breaking Çeda's hold, and soon he was on top of *her*, holding her kenshar across her throat.

Before he could use it a dark line swept down over Çeda's field of vision. Kadir was suddenly behind Makuo, holding two wooden handles to which the ends of a thin but sturdy wire were attached. As the wire tightened around Makuo's neck, a form darkened the doorway to Çeda's right.

"No!"

Hidi, holding the knife he'd been using to torture Rü-mayesh these past many months, charged Kadir. So fix-ated was he on saving his brother, though, that he didn't see Çeda as she used her legs to trap one of his. She twisted her body and brought him to the floor. Hidi fell hard. His knife slipped from his grasp, skittering away and clanging against the foot of a golden mirror.

Gurgling sounds came from Makuo as he stabbed backward, catching Kadir once across his shoulder and again on his forearm. But Kadir had his knee against Ma-kuo's upper back and was sawing the dark wire back and forth. There was blood all along Makuo's neck. Makuo, desperate, dropped the knife and tried to slip his fingers beneath the wire.

But it was too late.

The wire slipped further and further into his flesh, then slid with a sound of rending flesh all the way to Makuo's spine. A wet sucking sound filled the air as Kadir released the wooden handles. Makuo's dying form col-lapsed to the stones.

"Brother!" Hidi screamed.

He tossed Çeda away like a rag doll. He rolled, pick-ing up the knife he'd dropped, then advanced on Kadir with murder in his eyes.

But before he'd gone two steps, the wind in the room

changed. The dust and sand gathered, spinning tighter on some unseen axis until it had formed a cloud, had coalesced, had drawn into the form of a woman with cloven hooves, a tri-forked tail, and a crown of thorns. Rümayesh stood naked, eyes aflame, ebony skin limned silver in the moonlight. Her horns swept back like a crown, making her look somehow regal, like Goezhen's consort, a queen of the shifting sands.

Her form had coalesced just off Hidi's path. Hidi, sensing the tide had turned, sped like an arrow for Kadir, perhaps hoping to take Rümayesh's servant before *he* could be taken. But Rümayesh was reborn. She was swift and powerful. She was whole.

She darted to one side, grabbed Hidi by his neck and lifted him into the air, and though Hidi's knife bit into her shoulder, she slammed him down against the stone, his head crashing just next to the opening where Çeda had found the sigil stone.

In the far corner, huddling at the foot of one of the golden mirrors, was Brama. He watched all that was happening with wonder. One hand was dark with blood. The other held the sigil stone, the one Makuo had stolen from Çeda's pouch. Brama had written on it with his own blood. He'd written Rümayesh's name, her *new* name. The one that would give others power over her.

"Stand back!" Brama said, holding the sigil stone

before him. His eyes flicked between Kadir and Rümayesh. He was terrified. He'd seen death—all who grew up in the west end of Sharakhai saw death—but not like this. Not so close. "Stand back!"

Hidi was unconscious. Blood was seeping from his nose, from his ears. Rümayesh had been bowing over him, perhaps preparing to end his life, but now she stood erect and faced Brama. "What do you think you're doing?"

"Thalagir, I name you. Thalagir, I command you. Stand back and let me by."

Thalagir. Her name, the one Brama had chosen.

Indeed, Rümayesh tensed, her arms tightening, her hands balling into fists. Çeda thought surely she would defy him. After all, what were the words of a thief to an ehrekh born in the desert wastes? But to her wonder Rümayesh *did* step away.

That was when Çeda noticed the mirror behind Brama. As before, when Kadir was readying to step through, it wasn't reflecting the room as a mirror should. It was showing an image of *Çeda's* back, of Kadir's and Rümayesh's as well. Çeda turned and saw the mirror behind her. By the gods, she could see Brama's back through that one.

And then she understood. The portal had changed. Kadir was already running.

"Stop!" Brama called.

"Brama, behind you!" Çeda shouted.

But Brama didn't stand a chance. He looked at Çeda with eyes afire, as if he'd freed the fetters from a feral beast and no longer knew how to control it.

Kadir reached the mirror behind Çeda.

He ran *through* it.

Brama began to turn just as Kadir appeared behind him. In a blink he had Brama's arms. He wrenched them and Brama dropped the sigil stone. It clunked against the floor and rolled away with the sound of tinkling glass, coming to a rest at Rümayesh's feet.

Rümayesh picked it up, brought it to her nose, and sniffed the fresh scent of Brama's blood. A forked tongue slipped from her mouth, and she licked the blood on the stone. As she did, a shiver ran down her frame. Her eyes, however, were all for Brama. They looked at him with indescribable hunger.

That was when Çeda understood. The sigil stone. It bound Rümayesh, but it also bound the one who'd inked their blood upon it.

Rümayesh lowered the crimson-inked stone, took one step toward Brama.

"No!" Çeda shouted, taking up her knife from Makuo's dead fingers and running toward them.

Kadir released Brama and interposed himself. Çeda

tried to dodge past him, but Kadir was too fast. He grabbed her and held her around the neck. He avoided Çeda's knife, snatching her wrist and locking her arm behind her.

All while Rümayesh stalked toward Brama.

"Stop!" Çeda shouted. "You don't have to do this!" She fought, but Kadir was too strong, and she was still too weakened by the nightmares, by the constant lack of sleep.

Rümayesh shot one hand out, grabbing Brama by the neck. She leaned in and kissed him, smearing his own blood over his lips. Brama struggled for a time, but eventually he fell slack. And then their positions seemed to reverse. Brama stood taller. Rümayesh's form slouched, then collapsed to the ground.

Brama stared down at the ehrekh's form, but this was no longer Brama, she knew. This was Rümayesh. Just as she'd taken the form of the matron from Goldenhill, she'd taken Brama's now. Brama stepped over and pried the ehrekh's fingers from the sigil stone, then he turned to Kadir and nodded. Only then did Kadir release Çeda.

When Brama spoke, the quality of his voice, the cadence, had changed. "I thought it would be you"—she lifted the stone—"but one never knows where the fates will lead you."

"There was no need to take him like this."

"I beg to differ. He named me, and that, my dear sweet dove, is more than reason enough."

"*I* know your name now." It was foolish, perhaps, to state it so baldly, but Rümayesh had stolen Brama's form partly to ensure that her name remain safe. Çeda wouldn't leave this place not knowing whether she would be hunted as well.

Brama—no, *Rümayesh*—strode to where Hidi lay breathing shallowly on the cold stones of this room. She stared with Brama's eyes at the godling child, but her words were for Çeda. "It isn't merely the name, dear one, but the stone itself. Now go. As I'm sure you're well aware, there is unfinished work here." She hoisted Hidi up and over her shoulder, then strode from the room as if Çeda didn't exist.

Kadir made to follow, but paused as Çeda said, "You would have taken *me* when I came to save her?"

"You came to save yourself, remember?"

"You would mince words now?"

Kadir turned, a momentary look of shame in his eyes and in the set of his shoulders. "I would have regretted it, but my first duty is to my mistress."

"Does she not use you as she uses all of us?"

Kadir stared deeply into Çeda's eyes, as if he'd considered this question often and was still unsure of the answer.

"Is it using if I allow it?" he finally asked.

Çeda had no answer, and Kadir soon left.

In the desert, a league out from Sharakhai, Çeda stood next to a funeral skiff. Within the skiff was the form of a boy made with the sticks of an acacia, the holiest of trees in the desert. The form was shrouded in white, dried river flowers sprinkled over it. Vials of amber and myrrh and vetiver were gripped in the crudely formed hands.

Her crude effigy to Brama felt silly now that she was here, out in the desert, ready to bid him farewell.

But Brama was dead, or close enough that the distinction made no difference, and she refused to see him go unmourned. They might not have been friends. Brama might even have considered her his enemy for a time. But he deserved this much, a remembrance of the boy he had been.

It had been a week since she'd fled the keep and returned to Sharakhai. The nightmares were gone. Not that her dreams had been kind to her. She dreamed of Brama often, and she would wake from time to time, sweating, wondering where he might be, where *Rümayesh* might be, using his form. Was she back in Sharakhai? Would she remain? Would she keep Brama's form now that Çeda knew who she'd taken as her host?

Çeda had no answers to these questions, and they troubled her greatly, but as the days had passed she found her old energy returning. She felt almost normal again.

But that didn't mean she'd forgotten about Brama. She hadn't.

Çeda hoisted the sail and gave the skiff a shove. As the wind took it and it sailed away, she grabbed a handful of sand and let it drop from her closed fist.

"Bakhi grant you safe passage," she said, "and Nalamae kiss your crown, that you may find happiness in your next life."

Çeda watched as the skiff's tall sail dwindled in the distance, watched as it vanished beyond the horizon.

Then she turned and headed back toward Sharakhai.

Part Three

Bright Eyes and a Wicked Demon Grin

WEARING HER STEEL HELM, hidden by the mask of the goddess Nalamae, Çeda strode along the dark tunnel leading up to the pits. The white wolf pelt affixed to the helm flapped softly against her shoulders. Before any in the stands could see her, she halted, waiting for her name to be called. It was a day as hot as she could remember. Already, sweat trickled down her neck and along her spine.

In the pit ahead, the lanky Pelam circled, his arms gesticulating grandly as his booming voice recounted the tale of Çeda's time in the pits. In a strange turn of events, *she* was the one being introduced first. It had been well over a year since that had happened. When she was first learning her way around the pits, the crowds had known little of her. It had been natural for Pelam to introduce her early, holding the more renowned opponent, or the more intriguing, until last. But as Çeda had risen through the ranks of dirt dogs and won more and more matches, Pelam began calling her name last. Not today, though.

Today the pit would be empty when the White Wolf's name was called. And why not? She had to admit it created an intense mystery regarding the identity of her opponent. If the White Wolf had won so many bouts, then who was it that might outrank her?

When they heard her name, many in the stands began to howl like a pack of wolves. That was when Çeda stepped out from the dark tunnel and into the pit. The boiled leather straps of her battle skirt slapped against her thighs as she raised her hand to the gathered crowd. Many howled louder, especially the young Sharakhani, boys and girls alike. Others moved with money in hand toward the two men calling odds for Çeda to win. Others still simply watched, first her, then Pelam, then the door to the pit's underground tunnels, wondering who might emerge next from the darkness and into the intense sunlight.

"This day, my friends," Pelam called, striding around the pit like a peacock, head held high, one hand behind his back. "This day we have a special bout. One not seen for many years in these pits. The lords of our great city can often be found in the stands alongside you, spectators to the bouts fought within these walls, but rarely do they themselves step into the pits to bark and scrap with the dogs. Today, that all changes. We have one who comes from Goldenhill. He is young, but do not doubt his prowess! He is every bit the equal of the White Wolf."

Again the howls came. Others, the Sharakhani wearing the finest clothes, frowned, considering it brazen to support a fighter—even someone as popular as Çeda—when her opponent had just been revealed as a lord of the city.

"Our young lord has been trained by the best sword arms in the city, virtuosos in their craft. The young man is a prodigy. Or so they tell me. Presently, we shall determine for ourselves"—he waved one hand toward the door being rolled open by two of the pit boys—"for here he comes. Our own Lord Blackthorn."

From the darkness stepped a man wearing fine leather bracers and greaves. His boiled leather armor was well oiled and gleamed beneath the sun; a falcon with spread wings was worked into the breastplate. Like Çeda, his helm had a mask that covered all but his eyes, only his mask had not the face of a god, but a demon with an expression of naked rage. All of it, his helm, his armor—gods, even his bronze skin—was immaculate. Çeda was sure he hadn't fought a day in his life, not truly, yet here he was, standing in a pit after buying his way in.

Early that very morning, she'd come to the pits, prepared to take on an entirely different opponent. She'd taken the stairs down to the cool lower level and sprinted to the small dressing room designated for her use. She'd slowed, hearing voices, but then Osman had called to her from within the room. "Come, Çeda."

She parted the beaded entrance and found Osman and Pelam sitting across from one another on a pair of wooden benches. They were quite the pair, these two. Osman, a man whose frame was every bit as toned as Çeda imagined it had been when he'd fought in the pits himself, and Pelam, the master of the game, a man who looked like Osman's opposite, a man who'd break in half with one swift crack from a staff. Osman was by far the more imposing of the two, and yet it was Pelam who was the fixture in the pits, calling and judging matches, while Osman spent less time in the pits than he ever had, leaving more of the day-to-day management to others.

Osman motioned to a nearby bench. "Sit."

"I'd rather stand," Çeda said, wanting them to be gone so she could prepare for her match.

"There's been a change," Pelam said with a pinched expression, as if he'd just bitten into something distasteful.

"What change?" Çeda removed her niqab and set it on a nearby shelf. "I'm still to fight, aren't I?"

Osman shrugged. "We'll see."

From the chest in the corner, Çeda wrestled with the

canvas bag that held her armor. She frowned. "I need the money, Osman."

"Kydze turned up this morning with a broken ankle."

Çeda froze, her hands on the neck of the bag. Kydze was one of the best fighters to come out of Kundhun since Çeda's own mentor, Djaga. Rumor even had it she was a distant relative of Djaga. It was a claim Djaga assiduously denied, but in the way of these things her denials only seemed to make everyone wonder what she was hiding, and the more loudly she denied it, the more certain everyone was that it was true, making it one of the most anticipated bouts in recent memory.

Goezhen's luck, she didn't need this. She'd lost her last match, the first time she'd fallen in the pits. She'd pushed herself too hard, trying to recover from her adventures in the desert, hoping that by taking on another fight, she could make Brama's fate a distant memory. It hadn't worked. Months had passed since that harrowing night in Rümayesh's keep, and Brama's memory continued to haunt her, making her feel like a wobbling top, ready to tumble at any moment. Her birthday when she'd turned sixteen had been especially hard. When Emre had brought her a crown of jasmine from the bazaar, she couldn't help thinking of the crude effigy she'd made of Brama, nor the fact that Brama would have turned sixteen a week before.

"Why are you crying?" Emre had asked.

She'd held the crown and smelled its scent. "It's only, no one's ever given me one before."

Emre had rolled his eyes, but she had blinked her tears away, put the crown on her head, and kissed him on the cheek anyway. It had been a hard loss, but since then she'd managed to put Brama's memory to rest at last. She was ready to fight. She *needed* to fight. But now she would have to wait.

And yet, Osman and Pelam wouldn't be sitting here in her changing room, waiting to talk to her, if they had no other option to present. "What, then?" she asked, turning to face them.

"Several months ago, a young man visited me in my office," Pelam answered. "He came from Goldenhill, his identity hidden by a veil of rich blue silk, and he requested, nearly demanded, a bout in the pits. But before I could even answer he gave me his choice of opponent, as if I'd already granted his first request. I sent him back into the streets, thinking him some lordling who knew nothing of how to fight, but he's returned every week since, asking to be let in with, I'll admit, more tact than he had initially."

Çeda shrugged. "So let him. Surely he offered to buy his way in."

"He did," Pelam replied easily. "They always do. But

I thought it unwise in this case. He has the smell of the House of Kings on him."

"Then he has money to spare. Were you waiting for him to increase his offer?"

Without a trace of humor in his hawklike eyes, Pelam nodded. "In truth, yes. But I didn't suspect then that he might be the *son* of a King."

"But you do now?"

"I'm nearly certain of it. I had him followed. His residence is one of the elder dwellings, those nearest the wall circling the House of Kings. So you can see the trouble. I host him in the pits, and he loses . . . Perhaps dies . . . Well, it's the sort of trouble none of us needs."

"What does any of this have to do with my bout?"

"Our lordling came again this morning," Pelam said, "and this time he offered more."

"Much more," Osman cut in. He turned on the bench where he sat and swung one leg over the side so that he straddled it. He held a small leather pouch in one hand, which he upended, causing something bright and blue to fall into his waiting palm.

Çeda had never been impressed by riches. She found the ostentatious displays of the Kings both gaudy and vulgar. And yet she gasped as she saw the jewel that had dropped from the pouch, a sapphire as deep and blue as the desert sky at dawn. It was oval, and the size of a bloody falcon's egg. Before she realized what she was doing, her hand reached out to touch it. Though when she noticed how intensely Osman stared at her, she stilled her hand. "May I?"

Osman hesitated, but then held it out for her.

She lifted it from Osman's callused palm and stared. It was heavier than she'd imagined, and beautiful beyond description. More than this, however, was the fact that it was—to Çeda's admittedly untrained eye—free of the inclusions that most gems possessed. Gods, the sorts of things this stone might buy. A ship to sail upon. A *dozen* ships. A manse in the east end of Sharakhai. Food enough for a thousand mouths for a thousand nights.

Osman nodded his head toward the gem. "He offered this so that he could fight in the pits."

"*This* merely to fight?" Çeda shook her head. "Come, there must be more to it than that."

"You're right. There is," Pelam said. "As he's done since the beginning, he asked specifically to fight you."

Çeda couldn't take her eyes from the sapphire. "Me?" She turned the stone over, still trying to find some fault with it. She couldn't possibly be worth this. "Why?"

"We don't know," Osman said. "Have you made enemies on the Hill?"

The Kings, Çeda thought. *They're my enemies.* But that made no sense in this context. If they'd learned of her clandestine activities, they'd have strung her up by now, not sent some lordling in the small hope that he'd be able to maul her in the pits.

"None that I'm aware of," she replied, then worked some of the other implications through. "You don't think Kydze . . . Her broken ankle."

Osman shrugged. "Nothing we can prove, of course, but it does seem to be awfully convenient timing, does it not?"

By Tulathan's bright smile, she knew she'd gained some notoriety since entering the pits—she'd won all but one of her eleven bouts so far—but to have a man, perhaps a son of the Kings themselves, come to the pits and offer a jewel like this to have the honor of standing across from her, to harm Çeda's scheduled opponent so that Osman might feel added pressure . . .

"And what did you tell him?" Çeda asked.

At this, Osman stood and took the sapphire from her hand. "This is all strange enough that I'm giving the option to you. Decline, and I'll tell him to steer his tight little backside back toward Goldenhill where it belongs."

"With a bit more tact than that," Pelam put in.

Osman glanced at him sidelong, a wry grin on his face. "But should you accept"—Osman held up the gem—"then part of this is yours."

The gem twinkled in the lantern light.

"How much of it?" she asked.

"A hundred rahl."

Gods, a hundred rahl. A century of golden coins. She'd never seen so much in her life. But there was more to it than simple coin. The sapphire proved how desperate this man was to fight her; she found herself wanting to agree just to deny him the win. This prat from the east end of Sharakhai thought he could come here and steal glory from her? Perhaps a bit of pride while he was at it?

"You don't mind if I leave him crying on the pit floor do you?"

Osman smiled. "I don't mind one bit. In fact"—he dropped the sapphire into its leather pouch and cinched it tight—"I'd be disappointed if you didn't."

In the pit, Çeda watched the Lord Blackthorn preen before the crowd. She hadn't thought it possible, but it made her even *more* desperate to grind his face into the dirt. She found herself bouncing on the balls of her feet, a thing her mentor, Djaga, had tried again and again to beat out of her. For the most part she had, but there were days like this when Çeda couldn't wait to begin. They must be quite the sight, the two of them, a highborn lord and a girl who'd risen from the slums, their identities hidden behind their armor. Even Çeda was not immune to the poetry of it all; were she in the stands, she'd be watching rapt as well.

Çeda was given first choice of weapons. She chose a

three-section staff, after which her opponent chose a simple fighting staff. He swung it over his head, around his back, in a dizzying series of useless moves meant only to impress the crowd. And it did. Gasps came. Many moved closer to the front, jockeying for position.

The betting had died down. The crowd fell into an eager silence, glances alternating between Çeda and Pelam and Blackthorn. Pelam held out his gong. He paused as the tension crescendoed, bringing the crowd to utter silence. Then he struck the gong once and backed quickly away.

Çeda pretended she was ready to rush in, but then stopped and unleashed a series of moves aimed at his head, then legs, then head again. Blackthorn blocked the chained sections of her staff easily, keeping careful distance. Holding one end of her three-section staff, she gave ground to avoid a strike to the ribs, then countered. He blocked, catching the mid-section of her staff, at which point Çeda snapped the end she was holding. The movement caused the farthest section to whip inward, and it caught Blackthorn across the helmet. It had little power behind it, but the crowd loved it. They stamped their feet and shook their fists.

If Blackthorn was angry, she couldn't sense it in his movements. He remained composed, even as she managed to use the move again, this time striking his shoulder, and a third time, connecting with his knee, a sharper blow that sent him hobbling backward for a moment. Each time it happened, the crowd roared louder, both eager, and not, for the end of the bout.

Blackthorn pressed, but he was playing into Çeda's strengths. She was a patient fighter. She had to be. Too many of her opponents were larger and stronger, so she'd reined in her impatience, and with Djaga's help had learned how to make it seem as though she were pressing without actually doing so.

Blackthorn's staff became a hummingbird, darting in over and over. Çeda blocked, retreated, twisted away, and riposted. She struck him again and again—light hits only, but he was becoming defensive. She disguised her next move well, leaving her defenses low to bait him. He tried a few simple snaps of his staff toward her head, blows she blocked, but then he struck low and reversed, putting his weight and brawn into the swing.

Stepping just outside the arc of the downward swing, she caught the top of his staff in the short chain between two sections of her own. She twisted the ends, catching the staff in a vice-like grip between the steel caps and chain. She dove forward and rolled, wrenching the staff away from him. She realized well too late that he'd been prepared to lose his weapon, that he'd likely been ready for the whole gambit.

As she was rolling away, she saw him launch himself

toward her even as his staff twisted away. He snatched her left wrist, then snaked behind her. She tried to keep her momentum, tried to roll again, even with him draped across her back, hoping to twist out of his grasp. But again he was ready for it, and soon they came to a stop, his arm around her neck as he craned her body backward.

"Well, well, well, Çedamihn. Had I known you were *this* good I daresay I might have arranged to come sooner."

Gods, that voice.

The words had come out strangely slurred, but she knew as she knew her own name that this was Brama, the thief she'd taken with her to save Rümayesh. When she'd seen him last, he'd just written his blood on a piece of obsidian, one that had given Rümayesh new life, and Rümayesh had repaid him by possessing him, stealing his form with the help of her most loyal servant, Kadir.

She searched the stands as the rush of her own blood filled her ears. She found him moments later. Kadir, standing three rows up, the lone spectator who wasn't shouting or staring with an exhilarated expression. In fact, he was calm itself, as if everything so far had gone according to his master's plans.

Her mind spun with the implications. Brama was no lord from Goldenhill, but surely with Rümayesh's resources, not to mention the spells she might conjure, he could have bought his way into a lord's good graces, perhaps convincing him that he was some long lost cousin who'd come to Sharakhai, a prince in his own right in one of the many desert tribes. It wouldn't be so difficult for an ehrekh to weave any tale she wished.

"Why?" was all she managed to ask.

"Why does the spider hunt the fly?" Rümayesh said with Brama's voice. "Why does the snake pursue the vole?"

The answer was so blithe it enraged her, and she fought all the harder, heedless of the pain. She'd been caught in Rümayesh's web for months, and this after the godling boys, Hidi and Makuo, had toyed with her for their own purposes. The very notion of becoming enthralled to Rümayesh, of becoming little more than a plaything, lit a fire of rage inside her. She had little leverage, but enough that she could push backward.

Rümayesh was put off balance for a moment, but countered the move easily. "And what shall we do now? There's no need for us to fight for the pleasure of others. Why don't you come to me? Let us talk away from this place, and I'll tell you what my heart truly desires."

Çeda's answer was as clear as she could make it. She pushed violently backward, again catching Rümayesh off balance, then drove her legs like pistons, faster and faster until she'd slammed Brama's body into the wall of the pit.

She sent three sharp strikes of her elbow into Brama's ribs, then crashed her head backward into the demon-faced helm. His grip went momentarily lax. In that moment, she slipped from his grasp while slamming the back of her helm like a battering ram again and again into the mask of his helm. Then she bent forward, throwing his body over her hip.

He fell and rolled. His demon mask had come undone and now hung loosely from his helm. Çeda gasped. A rumbling came from the crowd as Brama's face was exposed. Everyone could now see that he wore another sort of mask entirely. The skin of his face, once so comely, was littered with scars—from burns, from cuts, she knew not what. She could hardly recognize the face of the boy she'd met by the riverside after he'd stolen her purse. Was that what had doomed him? It was no innocent act, but it had been the stone rolling down the hill that led to a landslide of events culminating in this: a boy possessed by an ehrekh, tortured even while she inhabited him.

"As the gods live and breathe, why?" Çeda asked, ignoring the strange silence of the crowd.

"Because he fought, dear girl," Rümayesh said from Brama's ruined lips, "and the same will happen to you if *you* resist."

The crowd grumbled. Pelam had been watching this

exchange with concern, but now he strode forward. "Fight, or I'll call a draw and the glory and winnings will both remain in the pits."

Çeda stared at Brama. She wanted to free him from Rümayesh, wanted to beat the ehrekh from his body and his mind. But it didn't work that way. As far as she knew, nothing short of killing him—or Rümayesh's sudden disinterest—would free his soul. Whatever might happen in the days ahead, she knew she couldn't fight him, not like this. Not here. She opened her mouth to tell Pelam that she wouldn't continue, when Brama said, "I withdraw."

Pelam's eyes shifted between the two of them. "You what?"

"I withdraw," Brama said again as he stood. He used a finger to scratch behind his ear, an odd gesture, but then he blinked and nodded to Pelam. "The White Wolf has bested me this day"—he sketched a bow, moving his eyes to Çeda—"but perhaps there will come a day when *I* will have *her*."

His look sent chills running through her.

Pelam paused, clearly wondering if this were some sort of joke, but as the crowd grew ever more restless, he announced Çeda as the winner. While a strange, half-hearted mixture of cheers and whistles of disappointment rose up around them, Brama replaced his mask, hiding his scarred face once more, and now it was the demon that watched her, its face smiling, grinning, laughing.

Well before the sun had risen, Çeda waited with her back against a mudbrick wall, watching old Ibrahim the storyteller's house for any sign of movement.

She hugged herself to ward off the chill desert air. She hadn't slept all night. The realization that Rümayesh had returned, and that she'd set her sights on Çeda once again, had been gnawing at her like a rat trapped inside her skull.

She couldn't get those scars out of her mind. There had been so many, some old, some new. And they were so horrific. Somehow she knew that Brama had felt it all, and that Rümayesh had enjoyed his pain. Why she would be so sadistic toward him, Çeda had no idea. The ehrekh were not like the men and women of the desert. They were covetous things, crafted by the hand of a wicked god. It was said that each had been made by Goezhen himself, and that their personalities had been influenced by the mood of the god of chaos at the time of their creation. Some few were benevolent spirits, created when Goezhen was in a rare, charitable mood. Others were tricksters, inheriting the mischievous traits Goezhen was sometimes known for. A good many, however, were vicious and sadistic, the qualities most often attributed to Goezhen, and it took no great amount of deduction to figure which flavor Goezhen had served up when he'd made Rümayesh.

But why come for Çeda? And why now? Çeda had been there in the desert when, with Brama's and Çeda's help, Rümayesh had been reborn, effectively freeing her from the clutches of Hidi and Makuo, the godling twins. Makuo had died in that struggle, but cruel Hidi had been left alive, and Rümayesh had taken him, surely to enjoy her revenge in as many inventive ways as possible. Likely weeks or even months had passed before she'd finally tired of torturing Hidi and given him back to the desert. She may have felt some loyalty to Çeda for her part in defeating the trickster boys, but all things fade, including feelings of debt and gratitude. Wasn't that a lesson taught again and again in the old tales?

And now here she was: prey once more. But she would play the part of the victim no longer.

Somewhere in the desert, a jackal yipped, a sound followed closely by the laugh of a bone crusher, the rangy hyenas that plagued the desert. A scuffle followed, then silence, though who the victor might have been, Çeda had no idea.

At last, within Ibrahim's house a lantern was struck, making the interior of the small mudbrick home glow with amber light. She saw Ibrahim's crook-backed silhouette a moment later, the light dimming as he shuffled to the back of his home, perhaps to eat a bit of cumin bread, a bit of herbed goat cheese, before wandering through the city to collect coin for his stories.

Çeda stole around to the back of the house, then scratched at his back door. "Ibrahim."

The sounds of scraping came, an old man shuffling over stone tiles. The door opened, and Çeda squinted from the suddenly bright light of the lantern he held in one hand.

"Who's there?"

This came not from Ibrahim, but from the shadowed form of a woman standing deeper in their home.

"Back to bed, my love. It's only a lost little wren."

"Don't forget your limes today."

"I won't," Ibrahim replied.

"It helps with the gout."

"I won't forget," he repeated, his annoyance poorly concealed, and the dark form receded like an appeased revenant. Ibrahim turned back to Çeda and waved her in. "Come."

"It would be better if we spoke outside."

"I'll not speak without my tea." Ibrahim glanced back toward the open doorway, then whispered, "As well as my lime."

He motioned her to a table with three chairs around

it. The mosaic worked into the tabletop—an amberlark, its wings spread wide—reminded Çeda of Blackthorn's armor. She sat as Ibrahim stoked the coals in the potbellied stove and poured water into a copper kettle. He worked in silence, and for a time Çeda was glad for it. Her mind had been a fire running wild, each fear fanning the next, like embers on the wind, steadily widening the blaze. Seeing Ibrahim go through this simple morning ritual, and the smell of the fermented tea leaves as they steeped, gave her a sense of normalcy. She knew it to be false, and yet it was a place of calm, a respite from the storm, so that by the time Ibrahim set a cup of steaming, jasmine-scented tea before her, she actually hoped she might be able to do something about this.

After setting down his own cup of tea, and a small plate with a lime cut in two, Ibrahim squeezed one of the lime halves into his own tea and the other into hers. She was about to protest when he leaned down and shushed her. "It helps with the gout." That done, he lowered himself into an empty chair, cradled his teacup in both hands, and regarded Çeda with expressive eyes and a gap-toothed grin. "Now, what can Sharakhai's oldest and wisest storyteller do for Çedamihn, daughter of Ahyanesh?"

Çeda didn't answer for a time. She held the tea to her nose and breathed deeply, allowing the name of her mother to tease memories of her first sips of tea years ago.

It was a sweet memory, more than enough to mellow the citrus taste of the brew.

Ibrahim studied her while sipping. His eyebrows pinched from time to time, but he said nothing. He merely waited.

"Do you remember when I came to you at the bazaar and asked you of the ehrekh?" she finally asked. As his smile faded, she continued, "I was being haunted by one in my dreams. I found her and freed her in order to free myself. I thought she might be grateful, that she might leave me alone, but now she's of a mind that I'm hers to do with as she pleases. She came to me as Brama only yesterday, in disguise, and said . . ."

Çeda stopped, knowing that she was moving too quickly, that Ibrahim wouldn't understand.

"Why don't you start at the beginning?" he suggested.

She wanted to. She wanted tell him everything. If there was anyone in the west end who might be able to help her, it was Ibrahim. "You can tell no one of this."

"It is between you and me."

"I'm deadly serious, Ibrahim. You can tell no one."

Ibrahim reached out and brushed his hand against her cheek. "There are stories and there are stories, Çeda. Some are meant to be shared far and wide. These are the stories that lift. That bind. Or that cause fear where we should be afraid. Those sorts of stories keep us as one and remind us of who we are. And then there are those that infect, that poison. Trust me to know the difference between the two."

Çeda swallowed, nodding. She took a deep sip from her tea, and launched into the tale from the beginning. How the twins had followed her, how she'd been pulled into a struggle between two women vying for Rümayesh's affections, how Rümayesh, in turn, had been drawn to Çeda instead. When she told Ibrahim of her dreams, they came back so strongly the room seemed to darken, and the cool breeze coming through the nearby window seemed to steal the warmth from her. She finished with Rümayesh's resurrection, her rebirth when Brama had marked the obsidian stone with his own blood.

"Brama named her—" Çeda began, but Ibrahim interrupted her.

"There was a day," he said, "when I might have wanted to learn that name. I was a curious man when I was young, *too* curious at times, but I've long since reconciled myself with the telling of stories, not living them."

Thalagir, Çeda thought. That was the name Brama had given her. How very desperate he'd looked as he'd spoken it. Just as Ibrahim had said of his younger self, Brama had been curious and ambitious, but he'd overreached and paid the price for it. He'd also saved Çeda's life. Had he not done what he'd done, Rümayesh would have possessed *Çeda*, not Brama, and *she* would have suffered everything he had.

"I only thought—"

"I know what you thought, but keep the ehrekh's name to yourself. Tell me instead about the fight in the pits."

She did, starting with the incredible sapphire Rümayesh had used to bribe her and finishing with the battle and its strange ending. "What I can't figure out is why she would pay so much just to enter, and then bow out when she might have won."

Ibrahim finished his first cup of tea and poured more. "What are sapphires but baubles to the ehrekh?"

Çeda shrugged. "True, but she's like a cat, Ibrahim. She enjoys toying with those she hunts. I know there are stories of the ehrekh, of them trapping men in jewels for a thousand years, of them using precious stones to draw the greedy to their desert lairs."

Ibrahim nodded, his eyes going distant. "Modern fancies penned by clumsy storytellers."

"Then what are the real stories like?"

"Who can tell anymore? Stories change over time, accreting new details like an ever-growing pearl that hides away whatever truth it might once have known."

"But you know many stories. Hundreds of them. Thousands. Stories are like glimpses of a distant mirage.

See it from enough angles and surely you'll come to see the truth hidden behind the wavering falsehoods."

A look overcame Ibrahim then, a fleeting thing, there and gone, but Çeda saw it: a look of shame. He recovered quickly, taking a deep breath as if he were considering her situation seriously. "Of the ehrekh, I know enough to know that they're dangerous, that they become fixated on things, as Rümayesh seems to have done with you. I know that they both love and hate man, for they yearn, as Goezhen does, for the touch of the first gods, and perhaps it is because of this that they so enjoy their games of cat and mouse. I also suspect that they are prone to overconfidence. Beyond this, Çeda, I don't know what you wish me to say. There is no magic I might give you, no bauble that might make the ehrekh forget, or make her cast her gaze elsewhere."

Ibrahim seemed worried. He didn't want to get involved. And who could blame him? If she'd heard some sad story of an ehrekh from someone she barely knew, she might do the same.

Çeda stared into her teacup, then took a sip of it to hide her desperation. It was fine tea, but it tasted so very bitter. "Of course," she said numbly. "I knew this was a fool's journey from the start."

She stood to leave, but Ibrahim grabbed her wrist. "They are creatures made by the hand of a younger god,

Çeda, and so are imperfect. Remember their nature, and
let that be your guide."

She nodded. It was the sort of adage that sounded
sage, but was actually meaningless, useless. "Thank you,
Ibrahim." She left his home then, into the cool morning
streets, and headed home.

The sun had nearly risen by the time Çeda returned to
Roseridge. She slowed, however, as she came near the
doorway that would take her up to the home she shared
with Emre. There was someone standing in her doorway.

The form stepped into the alley as she neared. She
pulled her knife, holding it at the ready.

"Çeda?"

He came closer, and she saw that it was Tariq, his
rakish handsomeness replaced by a haunted look Çeda
had never seen on him before. There were specks of blood
around his cheeks and eyes, and though the cloth of his
kaftan was dark, she could see dark, misshapen blotches
along the chest and sleeves. More blood, she reckoned,
but whose?

"What's happened, Tariq?"

"I need you to come to Osman's estate. Right now."

He took her arm and tried to get her moving back the
way she'd come, but she was in no mood to be treated so,

least of all by Tariq, so she twisted her arm away and sent a hard palm into his chest, knocking him back. When he tried again, she blocked his wrist, grabbed two fistfuls of his kaftan, and drove him furiously back against the mudbrick wall behind him. Now that she was so close, she could see his bloody lip and a cut along his chin. "What are you *doing*?" she hissed. "What's happened?"

"It's Osman."

"What about him?"

"He's gone mad, Çeda. I was in the yard, coming back from the stables when I heard him shouting at Sim and Verda." He lowered his voice. "He was raging. I could barely understand him. He claimed they were after his money, his fortune. Said he'd seen them going near his strongbox. There was a tone to his voice, like they'd stolen his own child from his arms. I thought to leave them alone for a time, let Osman work this out undisturbed. He knows his business, you know that." Tariq seemed to be trying to convince himself of something. "So I backed away, planning to return to the stables till it all cooled down, but then I heard Sim shout and go silent a bare moment later. Then Verda screamed, first in surprise but then in pain."

Tariq's eyes had gone distant. Haunted. She pulled him off the wall, then let go of his kaftan. "Go on."

"When I heard those screams I went to help, but

when I reached his parlor, Sim was dead and Verda was bleeding from a dozen wounds all along her chest and arms, and he was staring at *me* as if I'd been in league with them." Tariq swallowed. "The look in his eyes . . . it was murderous, Çeda. Dark, the sort you see on bone crushers before they bolt toward you, like he'd been possessed by a demon. I've never seen him like this. I've never seen *any* man like this."

"Osman's a careful man," Çeda said. "Vengeful when angered. You know this better than I do. So how do you know he *hadn't* caught them at something?"

"Çeda, he did the same to me. He stared at me with those black laugher eyes and asked me if I'd helped them open his strongbox. 'Why would I do that?' I asked him. 'For the jewel,' he said, and he charged me, grabbed me with his bloody hands and struck me and demanded I tell him where we'd taken it. And that was when I saw it, the sapphire. That gods-damned sapphire, just lying on the table beside his favorite chair. 'It's just there!' I pleaded. And Bakhi only knows why he decided to listen to me. He turned his head, and I saw his gaze lock on that stone, the lantern light glinting off its surface. That's when the animal look drained from him. He stood and staggered over to the table. He picked up the gem and stared at it for I don't know how long. I was too terrified to say a word. He finally turned and took in Sim, dead not two paces from him, and Verda, her blood leaked into a great pool in the corner of the room behind me. He looked down at his hands as if he'd just realized who had done the murdering. He fell into the chair, then stared at that gem, stared at it like it was the only thing in the world. 'Go find Çeda,' he said to me. 'Bring her here.'"

Tariq was seventeen, a year older than her, but just then he looked half that age, a boy lost in a city too large and much too dangerous for the likes of him. "So I've come, Çeda. He wants to speak to you, and I think you should obey, for all you owe him if nothing else."

For all I owe him.

I owed him much already, but now I'll owe him much, much more, for surely this is more of Rümayesh's doing.

Osman had recognized that, else why ask for her, of all the people in Sharakhai he might call for help?

She thought of all the stories she'd heard of the eh-rekh, how twisted they were, the games they liked to play. She felt like a fly caught in honey. The urge to flee was great, nearly overwhelming, but where could she go in Sharakhai to hide from Rümayesh? Where could she go in the Shangazi? Besides, she owed Osman too much to simply abandon him. At the very least, she would try to draw Rümayesh's gaze off him and onto her, lest more people she cared about be noticed and killed.

"I'll come," she finally said.

Tariq was visibly relieved. "Good," he said. He smoothed down his kaftan, running over the bloody spots several times, for all the good it did him. "Good."

With the sun now risen, Çeda took the steps up to the stone porch that ran along the front of Osman's rich manor house in the northeast quarter of Sharakhai. The servants, a dozen of them, all stood away from the house, some near the stables, some in the garden, all watching her as she neared the front door.

Çeda found Osman in the parlor, sunlight slanting in on the two dead bodies. They were just as Tariq had described them. Sim crumpled near the hallway to the rear of the house, Verda lying face up, hands splayed ineffectually over a dozen stab wounds.

"Osman?"

He was sitting in that chair, head bowed, the bloody knife lying across his lap. He was staring at something in his hands, and of course Çeda knew exactly what it was: Rümayesh's sapphire, hidden from view, cupped like a nestling in Osman's large, battle-scarred hands.

"Osman, you should come outside"—she waved toward the dead bodies—"let us take care of them for you."

"I've known Sim since I was a dirt dog, Çeda."

Çeda did her best not to let her gaze slip to Sim's

unmoving form, but failed. She took two steps deeper into the room, feeling as though she were walking into a lion's den. "I know."

"And Verda I met shortly after I left the pits, weeks before they were married in the desert." He looked up at last, but in the darkness of the room his eyes were hidden in shadow. "They were beautiful, those two. Together, I mean. Like lemon and lamb, Sim used to say."

"And Verda would always say no, like lemon and oil, grudging companions." She took one more step, ready should Osman do anything strange. "Why don't you come outside? See the sun. Breathe the morning air."

"I don't know what happened, Çeda."

"It wasn't you, Osman." She was by his side at last. She reached slowly down. She could feel her heart hammering like horse hooves in her chest. She reached her fingers between his hands, gripped the blue sapphire, now splattered with blood, and lifted it. "It was this." She held it in a beam of sunlight, allowing both the facets and the blood to show.

Osman stared at it, tears streaming down his face. There was worry there, perhaps some remnant of the fears he'd had last night that this treasure might be stolen from him, but as Çeda stepped away, he merely watched her, a look of deep sorrow on his blood-splattered face.

Finally, his gaze lifted and met hers. He shook his head. "It wasn't cursed."

"It was, Osman. By Rümayesh. You've heard her name in Sharakhai. You know her nature. What you may not know is that she's real. No legend. No myth. She's an ehrekh, and she holds the power of Goezhen in her hands."

His gaze held hers as if he was afraid to look anywhere else. "*I* held the knife."

"No," she said. "It was Rümayesh all along. *She* was Blackthorn. *She* cursed that gem. And *she* was the one holding that knife, not you." Çeda wasn't sure why she did it, but here was a man who had always projected an indomitable strength, and here he was, fragile, nigh to breaking. She reached out and ran a hand through his hair, as her mother used to do when she was young and afraid of the cries of the asirim on the holy night of Beht Zha'ir. After a time, she leaned down, kissed the crown of his head, and whispered, "This is all my fault, and I'm so very sorry it happened."

The rest Çeda left unsaid, but in her mind it was a damning refrain: *She was after me. She was trying to prove a point, that I can't escape her, that I'll do as she wishes no matter what I might try, that in the end I'll be cupped in her hands like a gemstone, powerless.*

Çeda held out her hand to Osman. "Come. The sun is shining bright. It's time you return to it, let it see your face, lest it forget."

Osman glanced to his right, to the sunlight as it played against the drawn curtains that were billowing in the morning wind. He looked back to Çeda, then lifted himself from his chair. The knife clattered against the floor, fallen from his lap. He ignored it, and took Çeda's hand.

By the time Çeda arrived home, it was midday and she was more tired than if she'd fought three back-to-back bouts in the pits. She collapsed into bed but not before hiding the sapphire in a small bag and putting it in the alcove hidden behind the horsehair blanket above her bed. Çeda had wanted to stay to help Osman, but Tariq had reasoned that it was more important to get the stone well away. Çeda hadn't argued. As she fell asleep, she tried to think what she might do, how she could free herself from Rümayesh's clutches, but all she could think of was the look in Osman's eyes.

She slept fitfully and woke only a few hours later, hungry and thirsty, so she left her home and wandered up the lane toward the bazaar. The sounds of barter and trade grew and then enveloped her, the embrace of a dear friend. It felt marvelous to be nameless for a time among so many other nameless faces—part of a grand collective but lost in the same breath. She came to a small eatery that served flatbread slathered with rosemary goat cheese and drizzled with a reddish oil that was as spicy as anything she might find in the bazaar. Under the sour look of the wizened woman who gave her the bread, she skipped over to the next aisle to get some rosewater lemonade, which they ladled into the drinking cup she'd brought with her. She wandered the bazaar for a time, watching the people from a dozen different kingdoms, melding with one another like individual flavors in some grand, sumptuous broth. Çeda envied them their lives. Most were oblivious to the ehrekh, or thought them little more than fanciful tales born of the desert they found so exotic.

Maybe she should follow Emre's advice and simply leave Sharakhai. Would wandering the desert be so bad? She and Emre had talked about it. They could both go, perhaps return one day when Rümayesh had moved on to brighter and more interesting baubles.

She'd no more had this thought than she realized someone was standing ahead of her. He wore rope sandals and a simple, belted kaftan with a hood that was pulled up against the sun. She'd nearly walked into him, and the crowd was so thick she couldn't yet slip past. That's when the face within the shadows of the hood registered.

Bright green eyes stared at her from within a ruined landscape of scars and still-healing wounds. "Perhaps we could walk awhile," Brama said.

It was still so disorienting. It was Brama's voice, but Rümayesh's words. He made a half-turn, as if waiting for her to join him by his side.

"You murdered two innocent people last night," Çeda said.

A woman in the crowd turned, but kept walking, eyes cast downward after she'd caught a glimpse of the man within the cowl.

"*I* did not murder anyone. I believe it was your *employer* who held the knife."

"After being ensorcelled by you."

"Do you know what that stone does?" Rümayesh folded Brama's arms across his chest. "It merely tugs on one's more basic emotions. Greed most often, but others as well. Anger. Jealousy. Lust. It depends on the man. If you say murders were committed, then I believe you, but I would look to the heart of the man who held the knife. Like a blackened vine, the heart is the place from which the foulest urges bloom."

"Love, too," Çeda said. "And kindness. And patience. And temperance."

Rümayesh laughed. "Perhaps, but tell me which of those wins out when man is threatened, when his fleeting life is nearly gone?"

"Many great things are created when the world is dark. Things of light and beauty made all the more so for the darkness that surrounds them."

With Brama's hand, Rümayesh waved to a stall across the way that sold mawkish, treacle-laden poems to the unwitting. "You can't believe every verse you read, dear girl." Rümayesh seemed suddenly interested in them, and began walking toward the stall.

Despite the desire welling up to pull the kenshar from her belt and stick it between Brama's shoulder blades, Çeda followed, falling into step. "What do you want?"

"Why, I want *you*, my little wren, but I've not come empty-handed. I can offer a girl like you much. A life of riches. A life without fear. A life filled with pleasure. All you need do is give me your heart."

"How could I ever do that after what you've done?"

Rümayesh bowed her head while staring at Çeda with a gleam in her eye. "You mistake me. I speak of a compact. One in which you do as I ask, and in return the rest of your life—your city, those you love—will go untouched. It will not be a willing compact at first, but when it is done, believe me, you will never look back. You will see only wonder in your eyes."

"I will see only what you wish me to see."

"You're quibbling. There's much I wish to see, that I would share with you. Be content in knowing that your

Osman will be safe. Your Tariq. Your Ibrahim and even your Emre."

The name hung between them like a bloody blade, all threat and malice and dark satisfaction.

Don't think of Emre. Don't think of Emre. She'll smell it if you do. "You say you want my heart," she said quickly, "but I still wonder why. Why not simply take me as you took Brama and be done with it?"

Rümayesh looked through the poems, many of which were hung from tall wooden frames, swaying in the hot desert breeze. She read a few, even pinched some of the frames between thumb and forefinger to keep them still before moving on. "When you saw me in the desert I was filled with rage. Knowing what you know of me now, you can understand why. I was perhaps . . . rash with Brama. I would not normally have done what I did. I haven't for a long time. But the twins . . . My heart was full of fire, more than it had been at any time since my awakening."

She stopped at one poem in particular. Over her shoulder, Çeda read it.

> *The soul is a flame that can never be extinguished.*
> *Blown by wind it may gutter;*
> *hidden by veils it may darken;*
> *and yet it will remain,*
> *waiting for all who seek it.*

Rümayesh soon finished and moved on toward the aisle between the stalls, but her hand caught on a frame. It slipped from its hook and fell to the earth with a thump, but Rümayesh walked on as if she hadn't noticed. The poet was a gaunt, dark-skinned woman who squinted and smiled as she looked up from her work on a new one. Rümayesh ignored her, and did something most strange. She reached up her left hand and scratched behind her ear. She used her pinky finger, a signal shademen used to indicate that a mark was home, but to beware, danger was near. Çeda realized now it was the same thing Rümayesh had done in the pit after they'd fought. Çeda had thought it a coincidence before, but to do it again? Brama would certainly have known such a signal, and it made Çeda wonder if there weren't vestiges of his soul that remained.

Çeda picked up the frame and replaced it, sending a look of apology to the woman. The woman seemed half confused, half annoyed, and then scowled at Çeda as she left and caught up to Rümayesh.

"To use someone in this way"—Rümayesh swept one hand up and down along Brama's body—"well, there's little satisfaction in it. It's like taking a hare by the throat. They scream when frightened. Did you know? That's what it's like. The sound of glass breaking. An incessant peal. But if you find someone who might join you of their own free will, the two of you become like one. You dance with one another. It's like a symphony, not merely beautiful, but a thing that resonates within your very soul."

"And yet you would be the dominant one."

They passed through a group of strangely short, light-skinned men who all seemed to be haggling at the same time with a carpetmonger. They came to the edge of the spice market, where a narrow alleyway at the back of a building met the old wall of Sharakhai. Çeda knew that it stopped twenty paces in. It was a favorite haunt of the gutter wrens who plagued the market and the bazaar. Today, though, it was strangely free of children. Rümayesh walked along it even though she could see it led nowhere, and Çeda followed, confused but curious to know what Rümayesh would say.

Halfway down, Rümayesh stopped. The two of them were cloaked in shadow now. She was staring at Çeda through Brama's eyes with a look that spoke of desire, as if Çeda were a dish she'd long wanted to sample. "In any relationship," she said, taking a step forward, "there is one who is dominant, but do not think I would control at all times and in all ways. There would be times when you will do as you please, and times when I will." She took another step forward. The two of them stood a hands-breadth apart now. "Very often, however"—she reached out and took Çeda's hand—"the two of us will join hands."

The moment Brama's hand touched hers, Çeda's eyes rolled up in her head. There was a feeling of her mind expanding, of its moving beyond her mortal frame to fill so much more. She felt the press of humanity moving about the city, speaking, haggling, arguing, holding one another, making love, meeting one another for the first time. The scents of fear, lust, ambition, and crushing depression came to her, but like the rush of the Haddah in spring it came in a deluge, a thing she had no hope of controlling.

There was a sense of something drifting through Sharakhai, a sense she'd never known. It felt old, like a rose sculpted from the stuff of stars, a thing plucked by the hands of the first gods well before man had set foot upon the earth. It was so beautiful tears welled in Çeda's eyes to run hot along her skin. The petals of the rose spread as Rümayesh leaned in. Its scent, a heady thing redolent of the tempering of the world, filled her senses as Rümayesh's lips touched hers. In that moment, something blossomed between Çeda and Rümayesh, a desire to link hands, that together they might rule this city from the shadows. It was a thing akin to love, akin to lust, like the moments of sex as one crested, though it was drawn out like thread being spun from a tuft of perfect, gossamer fleece. When Rümayesh pressed Brama's body to Çeda's, the feeling intensified, so much so that Çeda cried out in surprise and pleasure and something akin to pain.

How long she stayed like that she couldn't say. The span of a breath, the span of a call from a maned wolf baying at the twin moons, the span of a special meal spent with the dearest of friends.

When Rümayesh pulled away, she whispered, "This is how it could be." She moved to Çeda's other ear, placing one kiss before speaking again. "Should you wish to speak again, drop a golden coin into a well, any in Sharakhai you choose, and I'll be there before the ripples cease."

And then she walked away, footsteps crunching against the sandy street, leaving Çeda in that dead-end alley to fall alone from the heights she'd taken her.

Days passed. Çeda went to the bazaar or to restaurants along the Trough for food. She taught swords to her class of students at the pits. She attended the funeral rites for Sim and Verda. They'd come together from Tribe Halarijan, who burned the bodies of their dead and spread their ashes to the wind. And so that was what they did, allowing the wind to blow their gray ashes against the tops of dunes so that sand and ash were carried as one, mingling, forever traveling the expanse of the Great Mother.

Osman stood at the rear, away from the others, a place of shame, not by others' choice, but by his. Çeda came to stand by him after a time. They did not speak beyond mere pleasantries, but twice after the funeral she went to visit him, once at the pits and once at his estate. She wanted to see how he was coming along, but she didn't really wish to touch on the subject of the gem, nor Rümayesh. He didn't seem to, either. Both times he asked if she'd like some araq. "To honor the dead," he said, though she noticed just how much araq he poured into his own glass compared to the modest helping he gave her. He seemed ready to leave the subject alone, but as they were sitting on the porch of his estate, talking, having downed a second healthy portion of the anise-flavored liquor, he blurted out. "Where is the gem?"

"It's safe," she replied, watching him with care as the setting sun exploded along the western horizon.

"It's mine, you know, paid for entry into *my* pits."

She could hear the desperation behind the bullying words, and also the fear. "It's yours no longer. You gave it to me."

He looked ready to argue, but then he took a deep breath and looked around his estate, a beautiful plot of land with an old stone-and-wood house on it, a stables, even a small vineyard. It was the fruit of all his labor in the pits when he'd been a fighter and afterward, the place from which he'd begun to build his now-considerable empire. He looked at Çeda with an expression of gratitude. "And the ehrekh? Have you rid yourself of her?"

Osman had seen enough pain, and she hadn't yet decided what to do about Rümayesh, so she lied. "She'll bother us no more."

"Good." He nodded, as if the matter were settled. "That's very good."

More days passed, and Çeda continued on, waking, working, training, sleeping. There was a part of her that worried that Rümayesh would come for her. Surely at some point she would. But there was another part entirely that was petrified of the decision she had yet to make. She knew she was avoiding it, but the way Rümayesh had touched her. The way she'd made her feel. The memory had remained, like the aftertaste of the finest liquor. The very feeling was still so sharp in her mind, like she could reach out and touch it. Dear gods, that kiss. It terrified her. It made her want to run to Rümayesh to experience it again.

Twice she found herself taking a golden rahl with her on a walk. The second time she'd ended up at a well, staring down into its depths. All she need do was drop it and everything Rümayesh had promised would be hers. To touch so many, to reach beyond the boundaries of flesh and blood. To become like to a god. That was what

Rümayesh had offered and, gods help her, how tempting it was.

She'd held that coin over the well for long minutes. Tulathan and Rhia were high in the night sky. The coin glinted as she twisted it this way and that. She had but to open her fingers and all that Rümayesh had promised would be hers.

But then she saw the image of the King on the coin—it was too dark to tell which, but of course it was one of the Twelve who ruled Sharakhai—and she was returned to herself. In that moment she turned and threw the coin away, into the darkened streets. She saw it winking over and over as it caught the light of the moons.

As she breathed, blinking away the vision of the spinning coin, the door of a nearby oud parlor opened, spilling music into the night. The sound diminished as the door closed, but Çeda was drawn to it like a moth to a midnight flame. She entered and laid down money and drank until she could no longer see straight. She danced with a man who looked like Emre, but wasn't, the perfect companion for the night. She left with him and they made love on the roof of a packed tenement where he lived with his family and nine others.

She had hoped it would show her that Rümayesh was nothing, that she could live without her and have no regrets. But it only made her want the ehrekh's touch all the more. Laying with that nameless man, as pretty as he might have been, only served to highlight just how small she was, how enclosed, how trapped.

Had she her gold coin still, she would have gone straight back to that well and thrown it in. She didn't, though. She'd only brought the one.

But she had another at home.

She returned home as the sun was rising. She stopped in the entryway, the sitting room, looking toward the archway that led to Emre's room. How dearly she wished to speak with him. She hesitated, though. She didn't want him drawn deeper into this. He'd already come close when he'd helped her to find Adzin and the strange ifin in the desert and, later, Kadir. Still, she could simply sit with him, couldn't she? Perhaps they could go for morning tea, dine on pastries from Tehla.

She took one step toward his room but stopped when she heard something coming from the archway standing opposite his. From *her* room.

She walked in and found Emre sitting on her bed. The horsehair blanket above her bed was askew. Just next to him on the bed lay a small jewelry box, its lid open, and Emre was holding a clear blue gemstone the size of a falcon's egg.

Çeda felt her mouth going dry. "Emre, what are you doing?"

He looked up. If he was embarrassed at having been caught in her room he didn't show it. He merely looked at her, and then back to the jewel, as if he could hardly bear to take his eyes from it. "I . . . felt something in here. I thought it was you."

"That isn't yours, Emre. I want you to give it to me."

He swallowed hard. Licked his lips. He looked up at her, then back to the stone. "Where did you *get* this, Çeda? It's beautiful."

"I know it is. But it's mine. Now give it to me."

Emre blinked. "But you're gone so much. It's not safe leaving it alone. I could watch it for you while you're gone."

"Emre, give me that fucking jewel and get out of my fucking room."

His eyes lifted from the stone at last, cold. "Or what?"

"Or I'll knock you so hard your children will feel it."

He had no children. Neither of them did. It was an old joke she and he had told a thousand times—to one another, to their friends as they ran through the streets and the aisles of the spice market. She'd wanted to bring him back to who he'd *been*, not who he was now: a man holding a jewel that threatened to tear them apart.

Emre smiled. Then he laughed, flipping the jewel into her waiting hand. "Better put it somewhere thieves can't find it." He walked past her, then left their home. And finally Çeda could breathe again.

By the gods, this had been another message. The gem was cursed, and anyone near it, near *her*, would be affected. She thought of taking it out to the desert, throwing it to the sands as an offering to Nalamae. But the stories never worked that way. It would find its way back into Çeda's life and, sure as the desert was dry, fate would return with a vengeance. And even if it didn't, Rümayesh would still be out there, waiting.

Rümayesh had made a terrible error. For these past many days, the threat of Rümayesh doing something to Çeda hadn't seemed so dire, but the image of a spear hanging over *Emre's* head, ready to drop, had shifted something insider her. Shifted it for good.

The temptation of going to Rümayesh had evaporated like so much spilled water on the sunbaked streets of Sharakhai. Like a city catching fire, the feeling was replaced by a burning desire to give that creature everything she deserved.

By dark of night, Çeda strode into the small yard of Ibrahim the storyteller and up to the small porch of his mudbrick home. She held a book in her left hand, tight, like a talisman against evil. She should be tired, and in truth she hadn't been this tired since the nightmares of Rümayesh's torture by the godling twins, but anticipation and excitement over the passage she'd found kept fatigue at bay, at least for now.

She knocked on Ibrahim's door, knocking again when she heard no movement within. It was very early still—several hours before sunrise—but she couldn't wait. The time to be worried about manners had long since passed. When she knocked a third time she heard a groan, heard shuffling steps nearing the door. "Who's come to my door before even the gods have awakened?"

"It's Çeda, Ibrahim. I need your help."

"With the same problem you brought to me twice before?"

"Yes."

"Three is an ill portent, Çeda. It may very well bring your problems to *my* door next."

"Three is also a blessed number. Three times did rain fall when Nalamae touched her finger to the desert to create the River Haddah. Three times did Iri call before the sun awoke in the heavens. Three may free Sharakhai from the taint of Rümayesh."

His only reply was silence.

"I've found a story, Ibrahim."

The span of three breaths passed, then six, then nine. Finally the door creaked softly open. Ibrahim stood there, frowning, rubbing sleep from his eyes. "What story?"

She lifted the book and shook it. "A *wondrous* story."

Ibrahim's face screwed up as though he'd just stuffed a rotten prune into his mouth, but he left the door open as he shambled his morning pains away toward the kitchen. He lit a lamp from the oven's embers and set to making tea. When he'd poured a cup for each of them and sat across from her, he inhaled the scent for a good long while before speaking. She could see the worry in his eyes, if not his face. Eventually, though, his curiosity seemed to win out. He nodded toward her book. "What's this story?"

Çeda opened the book to a certain page and set it before him.

She'd found it after days of searching. She'd scoured the bazaar, gone to one of the more expensive bookshops in the city, pulled in favors to be allowed into one of the collegia's libraries—finding so much she'd paid a hefty bribe to stay another day and night. In the end, though, she'd found what she'd been searching for in a small, nondescript book she purchased in the Shallows. The shop owner and scribe was a woman who specialized in documenting stories from those freshly arrived in Sharakhai, those who'd come from the desert. The oral tradition in the desert tribes was vast, and many stories had never been recorded. But the woman had been documenting such stories for twenty years. She'd pointed Çeda to a particular book, which Çeda immediately bought and devoured that night.

Ibrahim ran his hand down the page. Then he went back a dozen pages and flipped through the entire story in as little time as it took Çeda to blow on her tea and take a sip of her own. *Nalamae's teats, no wonder he knows so many stories.*

"This speaks of an ehrekh being captured," he said.

"Yes," Çeda replied.

"Ehrekh aren't caught. They catch others."

"So the stories say, but now I wonder. The one who wrote it said it was one of the oldest from their tribe." Çeda motioned to the open book. "Perhaps *this* is the true story from which the others were born."

The story told the tale of a mage, the shaikh of Tribe Kadri, whose people were being haunted by an ehrekh. Night after night the ehrekh came, slipping like a dark shadow, twisting through tent flaps, ghosting around spears and swords, to take whoever it wished. They would hear the screams in the desert afterward, and though they ran to rescue the one who'd been spirited away, they would find only empty patches of sand, a bit of blood. Minutes, sometimes hours later, the screams would start again.

The shaikh prayed to Tulathan, for she had reason to

hate Goezhen and his children. Tulathan did not come for many nights, but when her moon was full, she came to the shaikh, who had affixed to his turban an incredible ruby as large as an eye, one of the treasures of the tribe. Tulathan took it from him, kissed it, and told him that he might capture the ehrekh when it came again if only he obeyed her word. He blessed the gemstone as Tulathan had bid him, and spilled his own blood in augury to learn who the ehrekh would come for next. He gave the ruby to that young woman, and that very night when the ehrekh came again, the girl held the jewel in the palm of her hand, and the ehrekh was drawn into it, never to be seen again. The ruby had been buried in the mountains shortly after, and the tribe never returned to that place.

Ibrahim's only response was to raise one bushy eyebrow. "You think this true?"

"Do *you*?"

Ibrahim shrugged. "So why have you come here if you know what needs to be done?"

"I've come because I *don't* know. The story doesn't say. I need to know how to perform the ritual."

"The story speaks of a gem."

Çeda reached into her shirt and pulled out a cloth bundle. She unrolled it and caught the sapphire in her hand. Even in the dim light of the lantern it was brilliant.

Ibrahim tried not to show his surprise, but his eyes

widened, his jaw worked. He swallowed, one hand reaching out for it, suddenly shaking, whereas before, while he'd been reading, they'd been steady as stone. "You said it was large"—his fingers stopped just above it, then his hand withdrew—"but truly I had no idea gems could be like this, so flawless."

He stared at it a while, but Çeda was growing anxious. "Well?"

It seemed to take a great amount of effort for him to drag his eyes off the jewel and regard her once more. "You want the ritual."

"Yes."

After one last look at the gem, Ibrahim sighed, as if with that breath he'd given up the hope of owning something so fine. "What the tales say of the ehrekh, how they hide the souls of man in such jewels . . . This story makes me think those might indeed be the same ritual. When Tulathan is brightest, one burns blood. Only the blood of man will do, as much as will fit in the palms of both hands. Burn it in a censer with the gem hanging above it. The smoke will coat the gem. When it's done, you will polish the largest surface with the wool of a newborn lamb. Show that surface to the ehrekh and it will be drawn into it."

She wrapped the gem up and stuffed it back inside her shirt. "That's all?"

"The stories I've heard and read are the same in this respect. Some others have the ritual performed deep in the desert. Others say it can only be done when the Haddah is flowing. Others still call for the gem to be buried in the sand for twelve days before the ritual begins. But they're all embellishments, I suspect. So, yes, if you mean to go through with it, that would be all."

"Tulathan will be full tomorrow night."

Ibrahim nodded, his eyes wary, worried.

Despite Ibrahim's fears, relief of a sort flooded through her, and with it came a deep and contented lethargy. Still, she was not safe. A river raged around her, threatening to carry her away, but she had reached a rock she could cling to for a time.

"Ibrahim, might I sleep here awhile?" She couldn't go home. She'd promised herself she would bring the stone nowhere near Emre until this was all done.

Ibrahim's forbidding expression told her all she needed to know. She was ready to leave his home and find a place in the streets to rest for a time when a voice called from the next room. "Of course you can."

Ibrahim's wife, wearing an ivory nightdress, her long gray hair unbound and flowing down past her knees, smiled at Çeda while squinting from the light of the lantern. "Come now, dear. You can sleep in my bed."

"I don't want to—"

"Shush, now. I'll have none of that." She waved Çeda to follow her. "I need to be up anyway. Ibrahim leaves early for his treks, don't you, my dearest love?" As Çeda followed her down the narrow hallway, she turned and whispered, "Can't stand the brightness of my sun."

"Can't stand the heat of your anger!" Ibrahim called from the other room.

To this she only smiled, ushering Çeda into her bedroom and the bed that lay within. By the gods, it was still warm. It cradled her like a mother would a newborn child. Exhausted, clutching the gemstone beneath her shirt, Çeda fell plummeting into sleep.

Çeda stood at the edge of a well. Since Ibrahim's, the day had risen and fled with the coming of night. Somewhere in the distance, an oud played over the Shallows, low and mournful.

She wore her black fighting dress. It was loose and easy to fight in while still protecting through the boiled leather strips sewn into it. She wore a black turban, the veil drawn across her face. Her shamshir hung loose by her side, a dear companion who'd rarely failed her. Wrapped in a cloth, secreted away inside a leather pouch at her belt was the sapphire, prepared as Ibrahim had said. The smell of the burning blood still lingered. She'd used her own, and truth to tell she was still a bit light-headed from letting so much of it, but she would take no other for such a ritual—Ibrahim hadn't mentioned one way or another, yet it felt not only important but paramount that it be her own.

Seven avenues met in a drunken rush here at the well, the center of a twisting, misshapen web of streets known as Yerinde's Snare. It was the most populous district in the entire city. The tall tenement buildings loomed, standing five, six, even seven stories high. Each of their low floors was subdivided into the simplest of dwellings— one-room homes that housed seven or eight each. Those who lived there slept cheek to jowl or in alternating shifts.

Çeda lifted her hand and unfurled the fist she'd held for the past half-hour. A gold coin glinted in the palm of her hand, lustrous beneath the gauze of the heavens, as if it knew how very potent this night was, as if it knew the part it was about to play. She'd held its sister not so long ago. She felt that same desperation, the seductive draw toward Rümayesh, but this night she was buoyed by seething anger over the threat Rümayesh had made on Emre's life and a sense that by the time the sun kissed the eastern horizon this chapter of her life will have been completed one way or another. With a glance up toward bright Tulathan and her gentler sister, Rhia, Çeda whispered a prayer to each of the goddesses, then dropped the golden rahl into the well. It glinted downward. She heard its distant entry into the water.

Immediately she felt something tug inside her, like the feeling of worry one gets when the truest of friends is in danger. She swallowed, turning from darkened street to darkened street, her hand on the hilt of her shamshir. Rümayesh had said she'd arrive by the time the ripples ceased, so Çeda knew if it worked at all it wouldn't be long.

There.

In the darkness.

A form walked down the street from the southeast. She'd guessed Rümayesh would come along one of the eastern avenues, but she hadn't known for certain, so she'd had Osman set traps on all of them. Thank the gods, though, they'd decided to station more along the eastern avenues.

Çeda saw them along the roof of one of the tenements, dark forms moving carefully. Something dropped toward the approaching form. Çeda closed her eyes just before she heard a soft thump. Then, as if a star had been born right here in the rough and tumble streets of the Shallows, a flash lit the night.

Brama reeled away, shouting in surprise. Shadowed

forms closed in. One clouted Brama over the head and he went limp. As simple as that. Like the snap of a finger.

"Breath of the desert, thank you, Osman," Çeda whispered.

After waking at Ibrahim's, she'd gone to Osman's estate and explained what she wanted him to do. Afterward, she'd handed him a leather pouch containing what little she'd managed to save after spending so much on Adzin and his ifin.

Osman had tossed the pouch into the air, weighing it. "What's this?"

"For your help. To pay for a crew. It's grim work, and those who come will need to be flame-hearted, no doubt."

"Grim," he'd said, tossing the pouch back to her. "Yes, I believe it will be. I know some who enjoy such work, and they'll do it gladly, but to offer coin would be an insult, for they loved Sim and Verda, even more than I, and they've come to understand the truth of what happened."

She'd been ready to argue, but Osman had talked over her, asking more pointed questions of what she had planned. She'd answered, silently grateful not only for his help, but for feeling as though she wasn't alone. Together they'd set up their trap. It had worked perfectly, and yet for all the simplicity of the act, Çeda knew their time was already growing short. Rümayesh would know something had happened. The question was what her response might be, and when it would come. Their fervent hope was that she would remain in Brama's form, that she might be incapacitated as he was for a time. But if Brama remained unconscious for too long, she might awaken and come to investigate herself, and that was something that would bode ill for all of them.

Several men picked up Brama's limp form and carried him down an alley. Çeda followed, twisting this way and that through tight spaces, until finally they reached a cellar. A waiting lantern was struck, and by its light Çeda could see Osman pulling the veil of a black turban from his face. Tariq pulled his off as well. Two others had come also, each wearing similar, threadbare thawbs and turbans. One held a kenshar with both hands, ready to drive it down should Rümayesh awaken. He was clearly nervous, though, for none of them knew if a blade would do any good at all against her. It might drive her from Brama's body prematurely, but that was the last thing she wanted.

"His feet," Çeda said quickly. "I need to see the soles of his feet."

Tariq pulled off his supple leather boots and his socks. Çeda looked there, expecting to find a tattoo, one that was meant to tell Kadir where the obsidian stone that kept Rümayesh's name could be found, but there was nothing there.

She waved to Brama's unconscious form. "The rest of his clothes. Take them off."

Osman's men complied, and Çeda looked over the rest of his body. *Gods, there's no tattoo.* "It must be here," she muttered.

She checked everywhere. His armpits, between his fingers and toes, the insides of his thighs, beneath his scrotum. She even checked the insides of his lips. But there was nothing. Perhaps Rümayesh had feared Çeda's knowledge of the tattoo and had changed her routine accordingly.

Brama's breathing hitched. He didn't awaken, but his head lolled to one side, exposing more scars along his ear and the side of his head. Some of the scars trailed up along his head, lost beyond his hairline.

His hairline . . .

"Turn him over. Quickly."

Osman and his men complied, and soon Brama was face-down on the dirty work table. Çeda ran her fingers through his hair, parting a section at a time. And there she found it, tattooed words, the hair having grown over it in time. Çeda pulled her kenshar, a weapon she kept wickedly sharp, and cut away Brama's hair in hastily sheared hunks. Slowly, the tattoo was revealed in its entirety: *In the temple of the forgotten lies a luscious bed of blue.*

"Nalamae's temple," she whispered.

"What?" Osman asked.

"Nothing." She nodded toward the men, indicating all of them but Osman. "Now, as we agreed."

"Leave us," Osman said, and the men left, but not before Tariq sent Çeda a look of hurt, betrayal. Well, he could brood all he wanted. She wasn't about to do this in front of him.

When they'd left, she pulled a locket from inside her black fighting dress. She pried open the locket's two halves and from within pulled out a pair of dried petals. She'd taken two petals simultaneously only one time before, after Hidi and Makuo had affixed them to one of the irindai moths. They'd helped her to fight off the moths' hypnotic effects and the will of Rümayesh. She prayed they would do so again.

After a kiss to Brama's forehead, she backed away toward the door. "I have to go, Osman."

"Not without us."

"No." She pointed to Brama, who was stirring more now. "As we agreed. Wait only long enough for me to get a head start, then leave this place. With luck, we'll all be far away by the time he awakens."

"And let him just walk away? He's not Brama, Çeda. Not anymore."

"I'm not going to abandon him, and I can't chance

211

that Rümayesh won't come for me in her true form. If she does, I suspect we're all going to die. You, me, Emre, Tariq. All of us."

Osman looked ready to order her to stay, to let *him* go to the temple, but he knew this was Çeda's fight, and that further involvement might be counterproductive to her chances of succeeding, so he simply nodded. "It will be as you say."

She returned the nod, and then she was off, into the night.

Çeda moved among the ruins of Nalamae's temple, stepping over broken stones, shining the light of her lantern over a grand mosaic. The mosaic covered the dome above—what was left of it—all the way down to roughly eye level. Above, the dome lay broken, the stars watching her, intrigued, expectant.

She moved carefully along the mosaic's pastoral scene, where a field of green surrounded a beautiful, flowing river. The scene depicted the years of bounty after Beht Tahlell, the holy day when Nalamae had touched her crooked finger to the dry desert floor, creating the River Haddah. It wasn't difficult to figure out what the message meant by *luscious bed of blue*. The deep blues of the Haddah's lively flow were still rich and beautiful even after the temple's long years of abandonment, but there was a *lot* of blue.

She moved slowly, knocking against the mosaic with the steel butt of her kenshar. She held the lamp to the wall in one place, her fingers atingle as she inspected a crack. She chipped at it with her knife, knocking out several of the square blue tesserae. There was nothing, however. No hidden hole, no cavity camouflaged.

She could feel the night passing, could feel Rümayesh taking steps on stolen limbs, coming closer and closer. She moved quickly, but not so quickly that she would miss the clues, cracks or discolorations, anything that would point her to the place where Rümayesh's sigil stone had been hidden. As edgy as the petals had made her earlier, she was glad she'd taken two. She needed the sharp hearing the petals granted, the keen eyesight. She needed their strength and verve.

As she continued, her confidence ebbed. She grew edgy, and then desperate, knocking harder and harder against the small squares of azure and cobalt and a blue turned copper in the ravages of the weather. She knocked more tesserae out. They skittered against the marble floor. Then she began bashing the steel butt of her kenshar against the wall, hoping, praying she would stumble across it.

Stop, Çeda. Stop. If you haven't found it yet, then there

must be a reason. Become desperate, and you play right into Rümayesh's hands.

She tried to take in the mosaic anew, lifting the lantern higher, then lower, considering things she hadn't bothered to examine closely earlier.

And then she saw it. A small home in the amber desert, hidden among the dunes. Near the home was a walled garden, and inside the garden was a bed of blue flowers. This was it. She knew it was so even before tapping the garden and hearing its hollow reply. She quickly pried at the stones, and in so doing saw the crack around it, and soon she had levered free a vaguely round piece of mosaic, revealing a small space where a black silk bag was secreted.

She upended it quickly, but before she could do anything more than verify that this obsidian stone was the very one Brama had used to change Rümayesh's name to Thalagir, she heard the scrape of footsteps behind her.

She turned and found Brama standing twenty paces away on the opposite side of the rotunda.

"You've done well," Rümayesh said, "but I think our game is coming to a close."

"Good. Then I'll ask you to leave me be. But before you do that, if you'd be so kind, I'd like you to leave Brama to me. He's done nothing to deserve this, and neither have I."

Rümayesh laughed. "What have any of us done to deserve our fates? Despite what the sagas say, it's all luck and happenstance, and occasionally the fickle whims of the gods."

"We're no threat to you."

"But you are. You absolutely are. You know far too much, and I can see now just how headstrong you are. You won't let it go, so neither can I. If you won't join me, Çedamihn Ahyanesh'ala, I'm afraid my own response will need to be quite final." Rümayesh took several steps forward and held Brama's hand out, a simple gesture that looked so very threatening. "So I ask you one last time. Will you take my hand? Surely you felt some of what I felt. Surely you were tempted . . ."

She took another step, a gentle smile forming on Brama's scarred face. When Çeda drew her kenshar and pressed it into the tip of her thumb, however, Rümayesh halted, eyes widened enough that Çeda knew just how worried Rümayesh must be that Çeda would wipe away the blood. Rümayesh shifted her position, coming no nearer to Çeda, but moving to see the hole in the wall. "You wish to name me anew, then? Control me as young Brama once hoped to do?"

"All I've ever wanted," Çeda said, "was to be left alone. Now, that's no longer enough. Nor is leaving Brama in peace. I want you to leave *Sharakhai* as well."

"And how do you suppose you'll force me to do that? With the sapphire? The stone I *gave* to your Osman? You'll find it an imperfect dwelling at best, dear girl. It won't hold me for long."

"We'll just see about that."

She poised the knife, preparing to press the finely honed tip into her thumb, when she heard the soft patter of footsteps rushing toward her from behind. She'd expected Kadir to arrive, and she'd known his penchant for the garrote, but still she hadn't expected him to move *this* fast. Something dropped across her field of vision—the black wire of his garrote, she knew. She had time only to lift her knife and press it flat against her neck before it was around her.

Kadir pulled the garrote tight. The sigil stone clattered to the floor, and Kadir kicked it with his foot, sending it skittering over the rubble toward Rümayesh. Çeda used what leverage she had, trying to push Kadir off balance. He held, but it was only a diversion in any case. With her knife, she sawed once. Twice. On the third time, the wire was cut.

Çeda spun away, but not before Kadir dropped the wooden handles of the garrote and backhanded her. Çeda reeled, and Kadir connected again, but only because she was more worried about pivoting to position him between her and Rümayesh.

The sounds of Brama's footsteps racing toward her filled the air. "Kadir, watch her!"

Çeda had only moments. She faced Kadir and feinted high, then sliced across his incoming fist when he grabbed for the sleeve of her dress. The moment Kadir recoiled from the pain, she lunged deeply, more than would be wise in a fight with a skilled opponent, and cut a neat line across Kadir's throat.

A river of red gushed from the cut. Kadir gasped. His hands shot to his throat, hoping to stem the tide of blood. He tried to retreat, but Çeda was already moving. She advanced in two quick steps and drove the knife into his unprotected chest. Kadir fell to his knees, his gasp mixing with a bubbling sound that came from the new wound. Çeda pulled the knife free, and warm blood gushed forth, coating her hands and wrists and staining the front of her dress.

Rümayesh slowed, then stopped near the place where the sigil stone had come to a rest. She stared at Çeda as if *she'd* been stabbed. "I would have loved you!" she cried. "Like no other, I would have loved you!"

Brama's scarred face brimming with rage and disbelief and sorrow, she bent down to pick up the stone, but her hand stopped just over it, hovering there as if it were too hot to touch. It took Çeda only a moment to understand why.

"No!" Rümayesh screamed. Brama's hand retreated, shook, then retreated more. "No! I will not be denied!"

Brama's entire body began to shake from the conflict within. He was fighting her. His desperation would surely be driving him, but already he was weakening. He couldn't hope to stand against an ehrekh. But he'd given Çeda time. As Rümayesh reached for the stone once more, Çeda sprinted toward him. It was four long strides before Çeda crashed her shoulder into Brama's body. His fingers had just brushed the stone, but now he was flying backward. His body fell twisting, sliding, against the dusty marble of the temple floor.

And then Çeda had it. Her hands were filthy with Kadir's blood, and she used it now to wipe away the sigil Brama had made. Thalagir, he had named her, but now Çeda was wiping away that name, making Rümayesh formless, bodiless, until she could take a new host.

Wind swirled at the center of the temple. It twisted into a cyclone, a body slowly forming within. Horns could be seen, a tri-forked tail. Baleful eyes and a terrible grin.

Çeda fumbled for the cloth bundle in her pouch, pulled it out as Rümayesh appeared in her natural form. The ehrekh arched back, spreading her arms to what remained of the domed ceiling, and released a bellow that sent the stones to shivering. "It isn't the way I wished it," she howled, "but I'll still have you, girl."

Çeda could feel the ehrekh's mind pressing down on her. She screamed from the pain of it, curling into a fetal crouch.

Then suddenly Brama was on Rümayesh's back, holding her arms, trying to contain her as he arched his head back and screamed toward the great hole in the dome above. Rümayesh's attack shifted. Çeda could feel the assault on Brama as well. It may have been this—Brama's will added to her own—that allowed Çeda to press herself slowly up from the dusty floor and with shaking hands take the sapphire out from its cloth wrapping. She gripped the smoke-coated gemstone in her bloody right hand, and then, releasing a cry filled with all the fury that had been building these past many months, stood and charged forth.

As she ran, one of Rümayesh's tri-forked tails slithered around Brama's right wrist. Another wrapped his throat. The third plunged into his back. Çeda leaped, gripping one of the thick horns atop Rümayesh's head, holding the sapphire before her eyes with the other. The only facet that wasn't clouded with the smoke of Çeda's blood now faced Rümayesh.

Rümayesh stiffened. A sudden heat washed over her. A cracking sound—like glass as the pressure upon it builds too greatly—echoed throughout the cavernous space. Rümayesh fell, and Çeda with her. The ehrekh's black skin became like ash, powdering as she tipped backward.

When Rümayesh struck the marble floor, her body shattered. Great chunks of her fell away. The exposed surfaces glowed like embers, but cooled quickly, becoming black, then gray, then white like ash. Her remains began to powder and flake. They swirled away on some unseen wind until all that was left in this forgotten temple of Nalamae was Çeda, Brama, and the body of Kadir.

Çeda looked about the expanse of the temple, feeling ill-at-ease. She expected Rümayesh to reform, or to wake in Brama's body once more, but nothing like this happened, and she heard only the frightening, rhythmic rasp coming from Brama as he breathed.

She crawled toward him. He opened his eyes and turned toward her, peering at her with eyes of emerald set in a ruin of crisscrossed scars.

"Are you there?" Çeda asked. "Can you hear me?"

He said nothing for a long while, apparently gathering his strength. When he spoke at last, his words tumbled out in one long slur. "You owe me two hundred rahl."

Two hundred rahl, the promised reward for helping her in the desert.

Çeda couldn't help it. She laughed, and Brama laughed with her.

In an alley not far from the entrance to the collegium medicum, Çeda waited. Dozens paced along the stone-lined street, some few glancing her way as she leaned against a wall within the shadows. The collegium medicum was a hive of activity, used by the sick, whether they had money or not, when they wished to consult with a physic.

When Çeda had carried Brama here two weeks ago, the attending physician, a black-skinned Kundhunese woman with expressive eyes, had stared dourly at Brama's gut wound. She seemed ready to set Çeda's expectations appropriately, but before she could speak Çeda took the money Osman had declined—the sum total of her wealth—and set it at the foot of the bed.

The physic had picked it up, weighed it in one hand, then slipped it into her belted white robe. "For the collegium," she told Çeda. "Now we see what we can do for your man."

"He isn't—" she'd begun to say, but the physic had already turned away, calling to an assistant, her voice cutting through the din of the large room like a scalpel.

Çeda had held Brama's hand as they worked, burning his insides with an iron brand and then sewing him up like a doll. Çeda had returned every day since to check on his progress. When she'd been told that he had awoken, however, she found herself unable to go to his room. She was responsible for everything that had happened to him; she had no business staring into his eyes while mouthing some piss-poor apology. Her words would be meaningless to Brama. Dust in a sandstorm.

"You're such a fucking coward," Çeda said aloud, to herself.

Three women, each carrying an ungainly basketful of bread on one hip, glared at her, but when she glared back, they frowned and continued on their way.

The morning ended and high sun arrived, and she wondered if the physician had been wrong. Maybe he'd had a setback. Maybe he'd died. No sooner had the thought come, though, than Brama stepped from within the shadowed halls to stand beneath the grand, arched entrance. He wore the opulent, blood-ridden clothes he'd worn when she'd delivered him here. His cowl was pulled high to hide his face, but she could see him scanning the street and finding her almost immediately.

Seeing no reason to wait, she stepped from the alley and made her way across the street, mouthing the words she'd cobbled together—an apology of sorts, though it sounded clumsy and patronizing at best, insulting at worst. When she came to a stop before him, her throat suddenly constricted.

The silence yawned between them. To say that it was

uncomfortable would be like saying merchants in the bazaar were moderately skilled in the art of negotiation. She knew she should say *something*. She just had no idea what.

"Could we walk?" Brama asked.

It didn't help her conscience that his words were still horribly slurred—also strange since it hadn't been so when Rümayesh wore his skin—but she nodded anyway, grateful. They fell into step alongside one another. Though Brama walked with purpose, he also walked gingerly, with the gait of a man on the mend. He wove them through the streets of Sharakhai, this way then that, clearly heading toward the heart of the city. Soon they had reached it: the massive circle known as the Wheel, where the Trough and the Spear and Hazghad Road and Coffer Street all met in a great, ceaseless cavalcade. They made their way steadily across the flow of traffic toward the grand pool at its center. Several hundred men and women—most from foreign lands—stood along the edge of the pool. Some marveled at the great, bronze statue of the shield and the twelve shamshirs fanned around it. Others braved the pool itself, walking with their trousers rolled up or their skirts pulled high.

Brama found an unoccupied space along the pool's marble retaining wall and sat down. Çeda joined him and pulled out a fine leather bag filled with coins, money she'd received from Osman only yesterday. "One hundred rahl."

He took the bag, weighed it in his hand. "Half," he said. "I'm well impressed."

"I'll get you the rest as I can."

"We might call it even." His voice was less slurred than it had been, which made her feel a tiny bit better. He looked out to the children playing in the water, as if he couldn't quite face her as he spoke his next words. "You freed me from Rümayesh when you could have left me to rot." Çeda made to speak, but he talked over her. "Had the tables been turned, I can't say I would have done the same for you."

"Well, I don't know about that"—she pulled from the pouch at her belt a bundle of cloth—"but perhaps this will even the ledger."

Brama took it as if he knew exactly what was wrapped within, indeed, as if he'd been waiting this whole time for her to take it out and show it to him. He unfolded the cloth, then stared at the smoky facets of the sapphire. Neither the stories nor Ibrahim had said to do so, but she'd taken more of her blood and burned it, covering the last facet of the gemstone, the one through which Rümayesh had been captured.

Nearby, a boy in the pool caught sight of the gem,

which despite the soot seemed to glow from within. The boy's eyes were wide as they lifted to meet Brama's, at which point Brama, his ruin of scars clearly visible, put his finger to his lips. "Our little secret, yes?" The boy swallowed hard, nodded, then rushed away, splashing water as he went. It was good to see Brama smile, but the look was gone in a moment. As he stared at the gem, worry began to replace the ill-concealed fascination that had colored his features until then. "Do you suppose it will keep her chained?"

"I suspect so. Until freed by the hand of man."

"Probably you're right. But why give it to me?"

"Because you know what's hidden inside. Because you won't be tempted by her. Because you, even more than me, will safeguard it"—she motioned to him, his torn face, his torn body—"so that this never happens again."

To this he merely nodded, as if it were not only what he'd expected, but *hoped* to hear. He folded the cloth and stuffed it inside his rich clothes.

"What now?" Çeda asked. "Will you find Osman? I'm sure he can find work for you."

He shook his head. "I don't know what I'll do, but not that."

"What then?"

"I don't know."

"You can come to me if you ever need help."

He stood and nodded. "Very well. Perhaps I shall."

Then he leaned down and kissed the crown of her head.

He took in the pool, the people gathered here. The look on his face . . . He'd grown up in Sharakhai, and yet his look was like someone who'd been struck by the grandeur of the city for the very first time.

He caught himself, seemed embarrassed for a moment, but then he gave her one last smile—a grimace on his scarred face—and strode away. The crowd parted for him like sand around stone. As he walked, more and more came between them—horses, carts, people, children. It obscured her vision, until at last there were too many and Brama was swallowed by the city.

Acknowledgments

This project ended up being the little book that could. I had no idea what would become of it when I started. I simply wanted to tell a few more stories about Çeda, a hero I'd become really invested in over the course of writing *Twelve Kings in Sharakhai*. The three parts of this tale each grew in the telling—a thing that happens to me often, it seems—but they also became deeper and more meaningful because of it. And I didn't do it on my own.

Thank you to Gillian Redfearn, Paul Genesse, Bill O'Connor, and Carol Klees-Starks for reading the early versions of these stories. Thank you to Marylou Capes-Platt, not only for copyediting these pages, but for putting a bug in my editor's ear about them. Speaking of which, thank you, Betsy Wollheim, for believing in this story and bringing it to a wider audience. Thank you, René Aigner, for creating such great pieces of art, and to Shawn King for your killer cover design.

I'd also like to put in a thank you to the gaming gang from way back when: Terry, John, Dave, Tim, Ty, Chris, and Brad. Thanks for all the fun times and for exploring all those new worlds with me. Little did I know, but all those gaming sessions were stepping-stones on the path to becoming a writer.